THE GODS
OF
WAR AND
DARKNESS

BOOK TWO OF THE IMMORTAL DEITIES DUOLOGY

NATTIE KATE MASON

Cover illustration and design by Bethany Gilbert
Interior illustrations by DECKYYURIADI

Copy editor: Chloe Hodge, assisted by Aidan Curtis
Series: The Immortal Deities, Book 2

For those who have stood by me from the very beginning.

Prologue

The God of War

'The realms have been razed in a blaze of darkness and chaos and I, The God of War, stood by and allowed it to happen. What the fuck does that say about me?

'The day I met her, my heart was remade and my world irrevocably changed. But who would have thought that a soldier and a handmaiden could have brought about the end of days?

'I was my father's faithful lackey. A loyal son and assassin for hire. Now, I'm a traitor to my kind and one of the Gods' most wanted. My father failed my sisters—failed me. Lilith and Nushka suffered through isolation, but despite it all, the mortal realms still flourished... Until now. All of them brought down in a matter of hours, thousands of innocent mortals and many of my own kind paying the almighty price for our choices. They didn't stand a chance...

'I followed my damn heart rather than trusting my instincts and the universe has paid the price. I fell for my sister's self-pity bullshit like a blind fool, and that weakness has caused the downfall of not only The Land of the Gods, but of all realms.

'No longer will I be idle. No longer will I watch as Nushka allows her hateful creatures to spread far and wide from The Pitts of

I

Moor. I will save my people with my lady by my side. Despite the devastation our union may bring upon us all, together, against all odds, we will fix the mess we made. With Lilith's help, we will set the world right.

'The only question is: how do two Gods and an immortal save the universe from the Queen of the Gods? It sounds like the beginning of a terrible joke, but it is the fate I have doomed us to. Life is about to get a whole lot more fucked up.'

Anastasia

It had been two weeks since the dark, billowing clouds and electrical storms had swallowed the horizon. A flash of light illuminating the sky revealed another wave of winged beasts raging towards Castle Brandistone.

The castle perched atop a peak amongst the Alearian Alps had withstood countless invasions, but it had never faced a trial such as this. Wave upon wave of an enemy never seen in this land had launched themselves upon the Kingdom of Alearia and, despite it all, she and her husband were still clinging to this life.

Water mages and fire wielders had battled head-to-head against the fire breathing creatures. When the winged beasts had grown tired of playing with their food, they had pierced their venomous teeth into the legionaries before tearing their bodies to bloody ribbons with their sharp claws.

A week ago, by sheer luck, Cimmeris had felled one of the winged snake dragons, referred to as *peuchen* by old folklore tomes. Shrouded in billowing dark clouds of his own shadow magic, Cimmeris had unleashed himself upon the peuchen, attacking it from behind while the beast was lost to the killing frenzy. Its severed head and body sent a shudder down the length of the battlements as the beast met its demise. A quick-thinking healer extracted the fangs from the beast with a dagger, in the hopes of developing an antidote to the venom, but such an experiment would take time—of which the people of Alearia were in short supply. It would not be long now, Anastasia feared, when the battle would be lost and even she, the famed Alearian shifter and hero of Alearia, would take her final breath.

Countless fathers, mothers, brothers, sisters, and comrades-in-arms, had been sent to meet the Goddess far too soon. Children were left orphaned from an enemy that haunted their waking nightmares. Such terrible loss and trauma. If those innocents survived, they would carry that weight upon their shoulders for the rest of their days. A fate Anastasia desperately fought to spare her own loved ones with each slash of her claws or crackle of her flames as she danced with death each day upon the battlement walls.

"Legionaries, nock, pull, hold! Wait until you can see the whites in their eyes, then release!" King Cimmeris bellowed towards the archers, pulling the arrow in his bow tight, his order nearly drowned out by the never-ending torrential rain. His Alearian armor, the very same that her departed father, the former King, had worn, was caked in blood and newly dented. Anastasia doubted they'd live long enough to see it repaired.

It had been two weeks since the weather had changed and the slaughter had begun. Two long weeks since the Priestesses had claimed the Goddess had turned her back upon mankind and begun to herald in the end of days. The Priestesses, who had previously revolted against the crown during her twin sister Annie's brief reign, had taken the opportunity to stir further discord amongst the people. Why they wasted their breath when they should be dedicating every moment to begging for the Goddess's aid, Anastasia didn't know. She had long lost respect for all Priestesses but the loyal few who served the royal family and had earned the Queen's trust.

Anastasia released a furious growl through the clenched razor-sharp teeth of the giant Shadows Peak wolf form she had adopted, in homage to her beloved's origins. She had given up shaking the snow and rain from her coat. The frigid cold mercifully didn't reach her bones due to her fire wielding gifting that threatened to snuff out due to her exhaustion.

She had shifted into her dragon form during the devastatingly deadly first day the Kingdom met its dark match, but one dragon fighting against a group of giant snake dragons was like a rejected lion facing off against an entire pack. Remaining in that form would have been akin to signing her own death warrant. It was only thanks to the castle healers' efforts that Anastasia had lived to fight another day. The thick, raised purple scars across her legs and abdomen served as proof of her brief dalliance beyond the veil.

Message after message pleading for help had been sent by raven, yet not a single ally had come to their aid—not even her beloved's kin, the shadow walkers. She feared they were battling their own unearthly creatures. If a people so formidable and gifted as those who dwelled within the darkness of Shadows Peak could not escape these beasts, what little hope did her army of legionaries have when there were so few magic wielders left amongst them?

The battle of Alearia five years earlier had decimated their legion's numbers and, in the time since, despite General Alecia's tenacious efforts, they had been unable to train enough new recruits to bolster their numbers. The formerly feared and formidable Alearian legion was now a mere shadow of its former glory. If the war continued for much longer, there wouldn't be anyone left to protect the vulnerable Alearian families seeking refuge inside the castle.

'For my family, for my children, I will fight with all I am and hold nothing back. With Cimmeris by my side, anything is possible. I will not accept that this is the end, despite what the Priestesses say. We have faced unimaginable odds before and lived to tell the tale, we will do so again.'

Steely blue eyes met her own fierce gaze. Sweat trickled down her King's dark complexion despite the frigid winter, Cimmeris's helmet long discarded in favor of greater vision. Her husband's shadows raged around him, preparing to strike at his next opponent. The one benefit of the weather was the overcast sky made it easier for the King to shadow walk from one dark space to the next—a rare, blessed advantage that worked in their favor against the seemingly endless waves of the enemies preying upon them.

"I will always love you. In this life and the next," Cimmeris promised so softly by her side that none could overhear.

Her heart clenched and she turned away from his gaze just long enough to blink back the tears welling in her eyes. It took all her strength to resist, for what felt like the hundredth time in the past few days, the urge to return to her human form and beg her husband to abandon his duties and instead wisp their children away to some long-forgotten corner of the human world where no one would find them. She didn't care what happened to her, so long as her children were safe. There was no greater love than that of a mother for her children. But despite all those thoughts of sending her husband and children away, pleading with them to flee this hell realm, she knew deep down that there would be no running. There was no one to flee to and nowhere to hide. The unanswered calls for help only reinforced her darkest fears.

Shaking her furry head to clear her thoughts, she forced herself back to the present. It would not do her or her people any favors to lose all hope. Besides, Cimmeris was no coward; it was one of the reasons she loved him so fiercely. He didn't abandon her in the battle of Alearia and even death couldn't stop him from leaving her side now.

'I love you too, with all my heart and soul,' she pledged, wishing with all her might that he understood her message through their soul bond and in the reflection of her silver-lined eyes.

As a child, she had dreamed of a love as strong as the bond she shared with Cimmeris, but never in her wildest dreams had she believed that such a love would find her. When she had first offered herself in matrimony to the shadow walker prince it had been to secure an alliance with his people so they might aid Alearia in its time of need. She had never dared dream of the love that would grow from their union.

Time was not on their side, and she didn't know if or when another chance would come around. She dropped her gaze from his, hoping that he had seen the deep burning love that she felt for him. The shifter rubbed her furry head affectionately against her husband's side and held it there for a moment as he cupped his unarmed hand to her furry cheek. The physical contact was as much an answer as it was to remind herself that he was still there, that he was real, and they still had each other. She would still thank the Goddess for that, if for no other reason. Though she wouldn't be surprised if the Goddess had turned her back on them for good. She had saved them once through Annie during the battle of Alearia, but Anastasia held no hope that the Deity would deign to save them again. The giant white wolf straightened her posture and lifted her head towards the sky, blinking back the rain that now stung her eyes. She picked her target flying towards them at an unimaginable pace and lowered onto her haunches as she prepared to strike.

Anastasia felt her sister's presence long before she first laid eyes on her as Alecia appeared from the arched doorway leading to the battlement's stairwell. Heat radiated off her thanks to her fire-wielder gifting. Alecia had barely rested since the attacks had begun. As General of the Alearian legion, Alecia had led the charge against each wave of the unfamiliar and deadly army at their door. Only when fatigue threatened her decision making had she finally conceded to Cimmeris's order to see a healer and get some rest. That was only a few hours ago—not nearly enough time to be effective in battle. A low growl built in the shifter's throat. She had lost too many of her family already, she could not bear to lose her last sibling.

As she approached her sister's side, Alecia tried and failed to hide the limp caused by a chimera bite to her lower right leg. Anastasia shot her elder sister a glare that could level buildings, which she conveniently ignored, instead focusing her attention on the approaching hordes.

The enemy was less than a mile away now, and the shifter's heart pounded incessantly. The Queen had foregone her usual evening calming tonics since the battle had begun, preferring to keep her head clear, but the anxiety building within her was becoming agonizing, like a smothering darkness threatening to tear her apart from the inside out. She would *not* allow her emotions to get the better of her. For her children, for her people, she would breathe and keep shoving her anxiety deep down as she focused on the battle ahead.

'I am the conqueror of my mind. I will not relinquish control or give my anxiety power over me. My family need me, and I will not let them down,' she reminded herself.

"She was given an order," the King fumed from Anastasia's other side, drawing her from her thoughts. The shifter huffed a low growl in response.

"I heard that!" Alecia grumbled, nostrils flaring, eyes blazing in anger. "Don't even start with me, Cimmeris. I saw the flipping healer and I'm ready to fight. I know my own damn limits!"

Cimmeris grabbed Alecia's iron clad arm, forcing her to meet his steely gaze. The General bared her teeth at him as she attempted to wrench her arm free, but he held firm.

"You're still limping," he ground out between his teeth, "and this isn't a game! The Goddess knows we need every warrior we can get, but if your fatigue-induced poor judgement causes you to make another sloppy mistake it could cost my wife or any of us our lives. It will be our blood on your hands. Is that what you want?!"

Alecia turned her head away, nostrils flaring, chest rising and falling deeply as she tried on this rare occasion to keep her temper in check.

"So, since you are obviously in no state to continue fighting, I suggest you turn around, get the heck out of my sight and get some Goddess damned rest! Do I make myself clear?!"

Alecia didn't have time for her customary smart-arse retort, as the next horde of deadly creatures made landfall.

2

Hyacinth

At the foot of a mist-shrouded waterfall, the remaining Wendigast witches made camp, a small fire providing a welcome reprieve from the harsh cold of winter. After spending a week in The Pitts of Moor surrounded by smoke, ash, and relentless heat with her departed kin, Hyacinth had returned to the land of the living to protect what remained of her coven. The Wendigast had served the Goddess of Blood and Bone loyally and many had paid with their lives—a cost that weighed heavily upon Hyacinth's shoulders. None of the other dark army's ranks had been hit as savagely as her own and a part of her felt great sadness for the sacrifice they had made to pave the way for their Goddess's allies.

Like lambs to the slaughter, the Wendigast had led the charge through a portal to the Land of the Gods. Their magic had bought the army much needed time to make the crossing safely, stringing up vast numbers of Gods and Goddesses with their grappling vines. She had thought them well prepared, but the arrival of the former King's pterocentaur guard—a trained legion of winged centaur armed with all manner of deadly weapons—had meant the end for scores of her kin. Had the invasion been handled differently, many of the formidable witches would still be alive today. Thankfully, Nushka had at least allowed her the chance to help her departed sisters transition into the Afterlife, an opportunity that had never been granted to her before.

Though despite Hyacinth's efforts the departed witches would mourn the loss of their powers and their proximity to nature until the end of time.

For the Wendigast, their blessed magic and affinity to nature formed an integral part of their beings. For their departed souls, it would be a mercy to cease existing at all. Unfortunately, the Goddess viewed their eternal appointments to The Pitts of Moor as a reward rather than a doomed sentence reminding her sisters of all they had sacrificed serving the Queen's *greater cause.*

Whilst Hyacinth was smart enough not to turn on the Queen of the Gods, she was determined to protect her remaining coven from meeting the same fate as her sisters. To do that, they needed to avoid drawing the Dark Goddess's attention or wreak enough havoc upon the mortal realms that Nushka would not seek to call upon them again. Hyacinth was a proud witch, and she would not be reduced to hiding in the shadows any longer, despite the risk.

After saying her final goodbyes to her departed sisters in The Pitts, Hyacinth had returned to the mortal world in search of her coven. At last, she found them at the base of a waterfall in the woodland bordering Alearia and Quillencia, a few hours upriver from a town called Lavender Grove. The fierce, endless storms overwhelming the mortal lands had made travelling increasingly difficult, a sign that the God of Weather was not faring well in The Pitts. This far south, the snow, thankfully, did not reach the ground, but the frost was killing off crops; many animals either went deep into hibernation or starved to death from the lack of food. The same fate would meet many of the poorer villages if their winter food stores did not last the test of time… provided Nushka's dark army didn't bring them to their knees first.

Most mortals had never heard of the Wendigast witches, a sisterhood of half-tree-spirit-half-witch race. Their identifiable branch-like limbs and spider-silk hair made hiding amongst the mortals impossible. Thus, the immortal witches had survived by hiding in the untraveled wilderness of the many Kingdoms. The few that did know of the formidable witches left sacrifices—usually the elderly or known serial criminals—tied to trees bordering their towns in the hopes of gaining protection when the witches were glimpsed gathering in their nearby forests. The witches gorged on the bounties they were offered, prizing the strength that the humans' hearts gifted them above all else.

Blood dripped from the witches' mouths as they devoured the remains of a young couple that had unknowingly crossed the coven's path. Their packs lay discarded by their mutilated corpses.

"My Queen," one of the crones said to the High Witch with a bow of her head, her breath pluming as she spoke. "We have an offering for you."

With a persistent tremor coursing through her hands, the hunched clan elder presented the two hearts upon a plate of bark to Hyacinth. As tradition dictated, the prized organs were distributed in order of rank. The leader was always gifted the hearts, the elders the brains and other vital organs, and the younglings were left with the entrails and flesh.

"Thank you, Tabitha," Hyacinth offered more politely than usual, her cold-induced temper dulled by the sight of the organs. One of the spiders that usually lived within her bark gown began crawling down her arm. Already salivating, Hyacinth snatched the plate greedily.

"You." She pointed a long gangly finger at a lower-ranking coven member. "Find somewhere else to be," she ordered, shoving the witchling aside so she could steal her seat upon one of the moss-covered boulders. The witchling scrambled away in search of a new place to eat, likely as far away from the High Witch's wrath as she could get.

The taste of fresh blood upon her lips whet her appetite, and she relished the rich, coppery taste. With each bite, she felt her power grow within, like a fire sparked from tinder. The first heart was just enough to restore her strength, but after gorging upon the second, she felt like a formidable force once more. Exactly where her strength and power needed to be to maintain her position of authority.

She sucked at the bloody muscle fibers wedged between her jagged teeth as she savored the last of the meal. It felt like an age since she had taken the time to enjoy her nourishment and two human hearts was a rare treat indeed. Goddess blessed.

After the meal was over, Hyacinth licked her lips clean and washed her face and hands in the stream, the current washing away any traces of blood. The smell of copper clung to the air and flies buzzed overhead as the few surviving younglings gorged on the carcasses, leaving nothing but bone behind.

"Sisters, our world is changing," Hyacinth declared, rising from her seat, the coven quieting at the sound of her voice. "No longer must we hide amongst the shadows. We are a proud race of witches, and it is time we ruled these mortal lands like the powerful immortals that we are."

Eager nods and wicked grins spread amongst the witchlings, the older coven elders raising their chins, smug expressions across many of their faces.

"We must be smart," Hyacinth continued, "and protect our own at all costs or risk extinction. We will not meet our demise under my watch."

Snickers and cackles filled the air. Several of the old crones saluted her with their goblets of wine in hand. Hyacinth looked down her nose at each of her kin, taking stock of the remaining witches.

"How are our supplies?" Hyacinth abruptly asked, impatiently awaiting a response.

Tabitha slowly stepped forward, the age lines revealing her centuries of existence despite the kidney she was in the middle of eating. She was one of the oldest remaining coven members and a loyal follower of Hyacinth since she had seized power in the wake of her mother's passing.

"Our herbs, tonics, and tinctures are almost out," she informed Hyacinth, her tone low and ominous. "Most of our reserves, as you are aware, were used to heal our injured upon returning to this realm. We have been attempting to replenish our stocks, but as many of us are not yet fully recovered from the battle, the newly-prepared tonics are needed just as quickly as they are produced."

"Very, well," the High Witch mused, drawing her mouth into a sinister grin, lips peeling back to reveal her jagged teeth. "Perhaps we will begin conquering these lands, starting with the quaint little town down the river. Quillencia is filled with gifted healers. I am sure our fellow apothecaries would not mind parting with their supplies."

Cackles and feral grins broke out amongst the group. Hyacinth straightened her posture, the thrill of the hunt building within.

*

The riverside cottage was a crumbled heap after being blazed by Wendigast fire. The healer had been permitted a generous minute to pack her things and flee—allowed to keep her life—whilst the elder witches had raided the apothecary stores. A magnanimous show of mercy on her part, Hyacinth felt.

Many pre-prepared tinctures and tonics would be welcome assets to the Witches' collections, and other ingredients like dragon heart string, which were usually harder to come by, were packed away. A younger witchling's hands and bark gown were caked with rich soil from pulling up the healer's herb garden. Such a wealth of apothecary herbs and supplies showed the level of care and experience of, not only the current healer in residence, but the outpost's previous occupants.

Screams filled the smoky air of the small country town as the remaining coven members rounded up unwilling organ donors with their elemental magic. The women and children were granted the kindness of being allowed to flee the village as the witches razed their homes. The young male farmers and blacksmiths, whose strength and youth were valuable, found themselves strangled by tree roots that ascended from the ground, pinning them steadfast against pine trees for safe keeping.

With fluid grace, Hyacinth approached the town square, her bark skirt swishing against the dirt road. At the center of the town stood a small, ramshackle temple. The building was in much need of repair, and it was clear to the High Witch that the town's Lord—whose manor was just as large as the town—deemed such maintenance a waste of tax money. The disrespect grated on Hyacinth's nerves.

Nearby, a quaint stone inn with stained glass windows, named after some insignificant knight, was being raided. The inn's liquor stores would keep the coven content for a time and, to show her gratitude to the owners, Hyacinth decided to allow the inn to remain intact.

"A grand feast will be held tonight, right here in the town center, to celebrate our coven's ascension from the shadows," Hyacinth announced. A roar of applause and approving shouts from nearby witches sounded. "Bonfires will be raised to warm and light the night."

Around the fires the more daring witchlings would dance and tempt fate.

"Rich wine will run aplenty and all of you, regardless of ranking, will be granted the privilege of gorging upon a human's heart." Gasps and excited chatter broke out amongst the coven. "The sacrifices are to be kept alive until the feast is underway. I want their warm blood to flow freely as we drink and eat our fill. The dawning of a new era for the Wendigast is upon us!" she cackled loudly, relishing in the moment. Her witches whooped in delight.

Hyacinth's personal guards followed her closely. Of her eight guards, only four of them had survived the battle in the ballroom. Four wicked souls, now banished for all eternity to live a powerless existence in The Pitts. The Queen of the Witch's second in command and head guard, approached her side.

"High Witch," Shahana began, her voice firm, "may I request a word?"

With a heavy sigh, Hyacinth turned her attention to her sister.

"Speak," was all she offered with a flourish of her hand.

The head guard bowed her head. "My Queen, we will follow you until we one day meet our wicked ends, but now that we have revealed ourselves, the guards were wondering what our future holds."

A feral grin revealing rows of jagged teeth grew upon the High Witch's face. "I was wondering how long it would take you to speak your minds."

The Wendigast warriors stood proudly and expectantly.

"Now that we have helped our dark Goddess take command of The Land of The Gods, it is time we claimed our own seat of power,"

Hyacinth proposed, her eyes sparkling in the firelight of a nearby burning building.

A menacing grin graced her second's face. "Nothing would make us happier, High Witch. Nothing."

"Then so it shall be…"

The God of War

Her breath came out in rasps as she grinded into him, the sounds she made slicing through the silence and his heart like a scythe. There was a time when he had taken such encounters for granted, but now, with the universe turning into The Pitts around them, Thorn treasured every moment with his new lover. This fierce, wild woman who had stolen his heart and his nerve.

"Agnes," he panted as he stilled for a moment to take her in.

Deep brown, soulful eyes met his own simmering gaze, and his heart skipped a beat as she smiled at him in that wicked way that was his undoing.

"I love you," she whispered for the first time, eyes alight, burning as she writhed beneath him, begging him to continue.

His heart hitched a beat.

"I love you too," he swore without hesitation as he unleashed himself upon her. Smooth, deep, hard stokes pummeled into her, the outside world entirely forgotten. All that mattered was their bodies and this fragile thing between them.

A cool, welcome breeze blew in from the balcony, fluttering the curtains and mussing his shoulder-length, sandy blond hair. Agnes wrapped her legs around his middle, drawing him even deeper. In the bedroom, this wicked woman was his equal in every way. She was wild and untamed. She hadn't sought him out for his title or power like the others. Instead, they had found and unknowingly saved each other.

"I need you," she whimpered, silver clouding her eyes.

He answered her pleas with each firm movement, worshiping her as she deserved, his tongue tasting her, *memorizing* her. He drew his mouth from hers and began exploring her neck, sucking, and then not-so-gently nipping at her ear lobe. Her answering moan undid him, and he hastened his pace, palming her breast and pinching her nipple as he pummeled into her, faster and faster, their breath catching, both panting as the tension built within.

A high-pitched groan of contentment ripped from her chest, his other hand massaging her clit as he pounded into her. His heart raced in his chest, faster and faster. Agnes panted heavily, her chest arching into him, and with a final scream, his lover climaxed.

He would never grow tired of making her happy. That blissful sound of ecstasy was like music to his ears. Agnes would be the end of him, and he would gladly allow it. As he free fell into bliss, with one final thrust, he roared as he met his climax. Panting, he collapsed upon her heaving chest, their mouths meeting, their kiss much slower this time as they cherished each other and drew out the last of their contentment.

Within the walls of his suite, they could be whoever they wanted. In this moment, they weren't a disgraced soul and a traitorous God; they were just two immortals in love with an unknown future ahead of them. A future that they intended to snare with both hands, but to do that they needed to first fix the havoc they had caused to ensure they had a had a life worth living together.

A knock at his suite door drew their attention and they both flung from the bed, quickly scrambling to find the clothes they'd shed around the room. Her silky midnight slip and his brown leather pants and white linen shirt were scattered over the floor.

"I hope you're decent," Lilith drawled as she flounced into the room uninvited just as Thorn hastily buttoned up his pants. "I have no desire to see either of you naked this early in the day. It'll spoil my appetite." She pouted. "Although…" The Goddess of Darkness paused. "I am intrigued to see what power you hold, Agnes, that has both my siblings so enthralled in your web."

Collapsing dramatically onto one of the chaises by the unlit fireplace, Lilith crossed one leg over the other. The weather was so perpetually pleasant in the Afterlife that the hearth was more for decoration than practicality.

"To what do we owe the pleasure of your company at this ungodly hour?" he asked, glaring at his sister as he pulled his tunic over his head, threading his arms through each of the holes, fully aware that his muscles were on show for all to see.

"Oh, please! It's almost lunch time and we both know I didn't disturb you from your *slumber*. The room stinks of lust and your seed," she smirked, her eyes sparkling in amusement.

Thorn sighed heavily, his head lightly throbbing. He surveyed the suite for a morning chaser to knock the edge off his hangover. The night's revelries had all been brought about by the wicked woman who shared his bed.

With her black slip hastily thrown back on, Agnes quickly made herself scarce, practically sprinting into the connecting bathing chamber to avoid the Goddess's taunting. The sound of running water drifted out of the bathing chamber, along with the pleasant aroma of lavender and rose oils.

Unable to spot even a thimble of liquor, with another deep sigh Thorn took a seat upon the spare chaise, propping his feet up, languidly bringing his arms behind him to rest his head upon.

"Again... why are you here Lilith?"

Lilith tossed the opened scroll at her brother. "See for yourself."

Thorn caught the scroll easily enough, his reflexes honed from years of training. Unfurling the scroll and beginning to read the message written in Nushka's cursive handwriting, he felt his temper rise with every passing line.

He tossed the parchment into the fireplace to use as kindling at another time, huffing in frustration before running a hand through his shoulder-length locks.

"I will not be summoned like a dog as our sister sees fit," he said. "Things have gotten way out of hand. We never should have helped her, much less fallen for her manipulative bullshit!"

Lilith leaned forward, crossing her hands in her lap. "You are not wrong, brother. We must act soon. The universe is falling apart under her rule, not that either of us should be surprised."

She conjured a cup of chamomile tea, from the smell of it, and Thorn a shot of whisky, which he gratefully snatched out of the air. After giving his sister a small salute, he downed the amber liquid, embracing the burn down his throat.

"Nushka has always had a flair for the overly dramatic. Much like someone else I know," she jested, narrowing her gaze at him.

Thorn ignored the barb.

"The title of Queen of the Gods is not enough for her. She has made it clear that anyone who crosses her will face their premature demise. A fact we must not forget. If we act too brashly, we will meet the same fate as the rest of our kin and will be of no use to anyone." Lilith sighed. Her shadows lulled along the hem of her form-fitting gown, lacking their usual vigor and curiosity.

The sound of the taps turning off and Agnes gliding into the bathing pool echoed. What Thorn wouldn't give to be in there with her right now, exploring her, tasting her. Devouring her little by little until she begged for her release.

Lilith sniffed, her nose crinkling. "Control yourself! Haven't you been sated enough already this morning?"

"Oh, mock me all you like, Lilith. You're just jealous because no one is warming your bed."

Lilith gracefully rose from her seat, abandoning her cup of tea on the chaise beside her as she straightened to her full height. She looked down her nose at him. "If I wanted to bed the riffraff, I would."

Thorn saw red, but before he could respond, Lilith raised her hand insolently, tutting at him. "Don't get your panties in a knot. I will see you in an hour. Let us pray to the stars that Nushka's summons is merely another of her pathetic power plays." With that, she floated out of the room, her shadows trailing behind her.

Thorn rose from the chaise and stripped himself bare once more. A moment later he was prowling straight into the bathing chamber to claim the woman who had so quickly stolen his heart and caused him to abandon all sense of better judgement.

The Goddess of Blood and Bone

Stretched out upon a bed of feather-down pillows beside her chamber's infinity pool, shrouded only in her shadow magic, Nushka furled her claws. Her hair slithered lazily over the pillow as Kayla, one of her handmaidens, tended to her. She had made a point of calling upon her more often after noticing the blossoming friendship that had begun to bloom between her and Agnes. It brought her great satisfaction to know that her actions would infuriate her former handmaiden.

After being granted immortality as a gift for helping her overthrow the land of the Gods, Agnes had dared to request that Kayla also be freed from her role to the Queen. Nushka had laughed at the suggestion, and it made the game she played with Kayla even more satisfying and intriguing for her.

Kayla's tongue and teeth taunted and teased, just as Nushka liked it. Beside them, two other handmaidens waved large fronds, the gentle breeze kissing the Goddess's skin. Nushka couldn't help herself as she began thrusting onto her concubine's mouth, forcing her deeper within, demanding what she needed. Kayla's fingers slipped inside and began pulsing where her tongue had just withdrawn. She licked and massaged that sensitive bundle of nerves that had the Goddess writhing beneath her touch.

Heat swelled within, her heart racing, breath quickening. She curled her index finger towards a fanning handmaiden whose name she did not care to remember. Abandoning her frond, the woman, dressed in the thin wraith-like cobwebs of the handmaidens' uniform, edged closer to the Goddess's side and brought her mouth down upon Nushka's breast. Sucking and teasing her, she massaged her other breast eagerly with her free hand. Growing restless, the Goddess reached for the new handmaiden, bringing her mouth to her own, whilst Kayla continued her ministrations, breathing life into her very core.

The second handmaiden grasped her breast roughly, rolling her nipple between her fingers, taunting her. Nushka arched her back, a moan of ecstasy escaping her lips as her core tightened while she explored the soul's mouth, embracing the frenzy of emotions that flooded her whilst Kayla continued to thoroughly devour her.

Rolling her hips, Nushka demanded more. Kayla pulsed her fingers in harder, quickening her pace and applying more pressure to the Goddess's clit, making her want to scream to the universe. Kayla moved, licking Nushka's thigh with such gentleness it sent shivers down her spine.

Nushka palmed the nameless handmaiden's breast, kissing her as if they had all the time in the world. The Goddess couldn't help the pleasurable sounds repeatedly escaping her lips as she finally met her glorious unleashing. Like a wave, the intense feelings of pleasure washed over her as she broke away from her maid's kiss. With a few final licks of Kayla's tongue upon her whilst her fingers pulsed hard and fast within, the Goddess reached her culmination, the balcony shaking from the unleashing of her shadows in response.

Nushka felt like molten lava as her limbs relaxed and her handmaidens silently retreated. She rolled onto her side, dismissing her souls entirely, and the Dark Queen took a moment to collect herself.

Momentarily alone, after taking another long minute to enjoy the warm sated feeling washing over her, she reined in her shadows to reveal her bare skin to the open sky, the sun like a warm welcoming caress. Gracefully, she rose from the ground and glided into the infinity pool beside her, the cool refreshing water reawakening her senses as she bathed and refocused.

✣

The Dark Queen, seated upon her throne of bones, looked down upon Thorn and Lilith with sinister delight. Her mother, stood trembling and chained at the bottom of the dais stairs, dressed as a servant. Nushka wanted to ensure that Aria received the proper humiliation she deserved before enduring the next phase of her punishment in The Pitts. Thus, Aria had been forced to be her personal chamber maid ever since her downfall.

Originally, Nushka had forced the Goddess to attend to her duties naked as an added form of humiliation. However, after the uproar from Lilith, who she was tentatively still allied with, Nushka graciously agreed to let the woman wear a uniform. Since the day she had claimed her throne, Nushka hadn't laid a hand on her mother—a feat she felt was incredibly magnanimous and far more merciful than the former Queen deserved. Her peuchen guards, however, had amused themselves by occasionally tripping the woman with their long tails or running a long, forked tongue along her limbs, causing the powerless Goddess to quake in fear.

The God of War glowered, his fisted knuckles white. "We are not your pets to be summonsed."

Lilith stiffened at Thorn's side. His clothes appeared slightly disheveled and the stench of his seed filled the room. Nushka straightened, her nose crinkling. The Dark Queen's hair flicked furiously as she tapped her claws against the arms of her throne. Her shadows slowly slithered down the stairs towards her prey.

"Am I not allowed to summon you? Is that not my right as your Queen?" Nushka asked, drawing back her top lip to reveal her sharp jagged teeth.

"You are not *our* Queen, Nushka. We were meant to rule *together*. At the very least, you and Lilith were meant to rule side-by-side."

"Is that so..." Nushka said, smiling sweetly, her claws now scraping up the arms of her throne.

Lilith glared at Thorn before schooling her features and taking a step towards the dais.

"Forgive Thorn, my Queen. He's only been fucked once this morning and clearly it wasn't enough," Lilith said. Her shadows moved frantically at the hem of her gown.

Lilith had always worn her heart on her sleeve, unlike the rest of their family. That inclination towards soft-heartedness had been one of the reasons Nushka had so easily been able to manipulate her in the past.

'A fool. A powerful fool, but a fool all the same. Goddesses cannot afford to show such weakness.'

"Lilith, my dear sister," she cooed, her hair now swaying calmly in the gentle breeze. "My followers have noticed you have been frequenting your former realm more often than is required of you. May I ask why? Are you not content in the Afterworld? You did request to rule over the realm. Have I not been magnanimous in granting your wish?" Nushka said, pursing her lips.

Lilith straightened as she looked down her nose at her sister.

"Do I need a reason to return to the realm I have spent an eternity guarding?" she replied bluntly. "The Gate to the Afterlife has always been my domain and whilst I do not wish to spend eternity there, I still place value on the role and the mortals under which I watch over. Do you have a problem with that, *Your Majesty?*"

It was as close to a snarl as the Goddess would get. Nushka delighted in the knowledge that she had touched a nerve.

"Oh, be my guest," the Dark Queen purred. "But be careful, or one might think you were visiting your realm to keep tabs on me through your clouded visions. I do not take kindly to spies." She was deadly calm as she unleashed her power, lashing at her sister with shadows.

Lilith deflected the attack, eyes blazing with fury.

"Do not treat me with the same level of disrespect as your sex slaves," the Goddess of Darkness spat, eyes narrowed. "*I* do not take kindly to having my motives questioned and I do not appreciate being spied on."

Thorn stepped in line with Lilith, resting a hand not so casually on the blade he had strapped to his side.

"Is helping you claim your crown not proof enough of our loyalty?" he said, knuckles white as he now clenched the hilt of his sword. "You have everything you ever wanted, yet you seek to question the only kin who have stood by your side."

Nushka rose from her throne and strode slowly and deliberately down the stairs towards her kin. Two younger peuchen moved to guard her flanks.

"I suggest you remember who you are talking to before my patience runs thin."

Thorn's nostrils flared as he growled at her, Lilith sneering at her in turn.

"If that is all, My Lady," Lilith ground out, shadows flaring, whipping at her back, "we shall heed your warning. Now excuse us, we have a realm to rule."

Nushka scoffed, eyes bright with malice.

"Step out of line again and I will have my guards watch over every move you make. You will not shit without me knowing about it. Do you understand?"

Lilith and Thorn radiated waves of power and fury, but they held back their retorts, mastering a level of self-control that she herself had never cared to work on.

"Get out of my sight. This is your first and final warning."

Lilith took Thorn's hand and together they vanished through a portal back to the Afterworld. The God of War raising his middle finger as he passed through the gateway, causing Nushka's sinister smile to broaden.

"Now we wait," she chuckled darkly to herself, summoning a glass of wine and drinking deeply.

Agnes

Thorn's suite erupted into a whirl of lashing winds and shadow magic, causing Agnes to flinch on the chaise where she was sprawled out reading a book. Lilith and her lover had transported back to the Land of Milk and Honey through one of The Goddess of Darkness's raging portals. Another glorious day in the Afterlife, interrupted by whatever nonsense Nushka had said to put the Deities in such a charming mood.

The chaise opposite hers upturned and smashed to splinters in the hearth, the linen and curtains of the four-poster bed ripped to shreds. Thorn didn't bother to dampen his temper as he stewed in his anger. Agnes tried and failed to suppress the eye roll at the magical temper tantrum he was throwing.

The Goddess of Darkness, groaned obnoxiously loudly as she magicked a new chaise to replace the now tattered one and flounced herself amongst the voluminous silk-covered cushions. A decanter of whisky and *three* crystal glasses, to Agnes's pleasant surprise, appeared on a small coffee table between them.

Thorn approached the side table with heavy steps and shot three nibs of whisky, before pouring all three of them heavy-handed glasses of the amber liquid. Floating on storm clouds, the extra glasses were delivered to her and Lilith. Agnes abandoned her book with a heavy sigh and caught her glass, taking a small sip as she mentally prepared herself for whatever drama was likely to unfold.

"We need to act now. We can't afford to wait any longer. That bitch needs to be stopped before there is nothing left worth saving." He slammed his empty glass down upon the side table before pouring himself another.

Lilith stretched her neck to either side before sipping from her own glass, legs tucked beneath her, gown and shadows oozing off her like liquid night. "Well, we have had no luck with our plan so far. *So...* short of hoping for a miracle, how are two Gods and one immortal going to overthrow our dear sister and her delightful little army of nightmares?" Lilith smiled sweetly at her brother, as she fluttered her eye lashes and peered at him expectantly.

Thorn rolled his eyes, downing another glass of whisky.

"Unless, perhaps, you *have* managed to achieve the first step in our plan?" Lilith pressed on, one eyebrow raised. "Though, judging from your temper, I would think not."

Lilith's emerald eyes brightened and her shadows seemed to move more hastily. Agnes could tell she was delighting in stirring the pot even further. Agnes, however, edged forward on her chair, her interest now piqued.

"What plan?"

Lilith smiled deviously as she rolled her shoulders and stretched out her neck. "The plan that involves raising an army of the dead to overthrow Nushka. Genius really, given the billions of long-forgotten souls at our disposal. You inspired the idea, actually! The only positive thing you have brought to the table since my brother decided to keep you around as his little plaything," Lilith mused. "But helpful all the same," she added, shrugging her shoulders.

Agnes bit the inside of her cheek, pursing her lips as she took several deep breaths in and out of her nose, resisting the urge to go toe-to-toe with the Deity.

"I'm so glad I could be of help," Agnes ground out. She turned to Thorn, choosing self-preservation over stupidity. "How do you plan to raise an army of the dead?"

Thorn lifted his eyes to hers, his gaze softening—apologetic even—guilt likely setting in after the temper he had unleashed only moments ago. She did not blame him for it, she was just as hot-headed as he was. She had been that way her whole life. From a young age, Agnes had learned when to pick her battles. She'd often suppressed that fiery side of herself to give the impression that she was a submissive, easily placated royal, rather than the fierce beast she truly was. Her mind was always ten steps ahead.

"Necromancy of sorts, amongst other things," Lilith interrupted matter-of-factly. "But that is none of your concern. Although... Nushka always did enjoy your *services*. Perhaps you could be useful as a means of distraction."

One minute Thorn was gazing into her eyes longingly, the next he disappeared in a flurry of darkness and re-appeared before his sister, pinning both her arms to the chaise on which she lounged, glaring with a ferocity Agnes hoped to never be the recipient of.

"Agnes is not some worthless toy for you to use as you see fit. Are we clear, Lilith?" His words came out husky. Deadly. "I will not allow her to suffer at the hands of Nushka again."

Defiant eyes glared back at him. Hands of darkness emerged from the Goddess and clenched their fists around the God's wrists, clamping down until the sound of bone crunching filled the room and Thorn was forced to unhand her.

"What the actual fuck, Lilith!" he swore, plunging his hands into a bucket of ice he had magicked from some pocket realm.

Agnes gasped as his mottled, bruised and disfigured hands reformed. She stared transfixed as bone snapped, one after the other, into place as Thorn healed at an astonishing pace.

"Touch me like that again, and your favorite part will be the next thing that my darkness breaks," Lilith warned. Her eyes ablaze with emerald fire.

Gracefully rising from the chaise and dusting a speck of invisible lint from her impeccable gown, Lilith glared at her brother once more.

"Call me when you have something to report," Lilith demanded and swept from the suite on a cloud of darkness, shadows irately trailing behind.

Thorn wrenched his hands from the ice water, shaking them dry, his bones fully reformed. Only his battle scars peppered his otherwise pristine skin, a tattooed sleeve extending up his right arm.

"Lilith is such a pleasure to be around. I have no idea how I have lived without her these past few centuries," Thorn said, rolling back his shoulders.

"As the saying goes, *'you can't pick your family, but you can pick your friends'.*" Agnes sighed and eased back comfortably again in her chair. "I can't wait to spend all of eternity getting to know you and your wonderful family more."

Thorn's answering smile was full of mischief as he strode towards her. "All of eternity, huh? I like the sound of that. Now where were we before my sister so rudely interrupted us?"

"Hold that thought," she said, lifting a finger to halt his advances.

"And why am I not permitted to ravage my lover?" Thorn asked raising a brow. She could see all the wicked thoughts ticking over in those deep, soulful eyes of his.

"I am not denying you—or *me,* for that matter," she said. "But before we tangle, can you please explain to me what Lilith meant by using necromancy? Are you both insane?!"

Thorn laughed. "Quite likely, but the only way to beat an army as dark and twisted as Nushka's is with one as equally formidable."

She massaged her temples.

"You're actually going to raise the dead?" she asked in astonishment. The color drained from her face as despair pooled in her stomach. "Have the dead not suffered enough? Do they, too, not deserve their rest? Have you forgotten that until recently, I was one of them? How could you think that I would be okay with this?"

Thorn moved to sit beside her, taking her hands in his own.

"It is not what you think," he replied, brow furrowed. "The souls in the Afterworld, will be offered a chance to fight for the peaceful eternity they deserve and for their loved ones still living. We will not force anyone to fight. We will only accept volunteers. We will raise an army unlike any other. An army of reanimated souls who cannot be killed or poisoned by Nushka's creatures."

"But they are just souls, they can't fight or hold weapons. It was only Nushka's powers that allowed her handmaidens—allowed *me*—to attend to her in fully or partially corporeal form. Only she had the power to return my life to me. How could the souls in the Afterworld possibly aid in this war? And why should they? Don't they—don't *I*—deserve that peace?" Agnes dropped her head and bit her lip, feeling as though the brief taste of safety and freedom she had experienced here in the Land of Milk and Honey was about to slip away. Despite her new immortal body, she felt fragile. Powerless.

Thorn cupped her cheek with a gentleness that threatened to spill the tears lining her eyes.

"I will never let anything happen to you," he promised. "You are mine and I am yours, and I will not allow anything to separate us."

She bit her lip as she choked down the sob threatening to surface. Staring into his eyes, she beheld the sincerity in his words, which only made her doubt why the universe had rewarded her despite her shitty human life choices. After all she had done, she considered herself undeserving and blessed beyond measure to have Thorn by her side.

"I promise you, we will not force this upon any of the souls here. But if we are to stand a chance at defeating Nushka, then we need all the help we can get."

"But even if you go through with this, how will you return their corporeal bodies so that they can fight?"

He dropped her chin, taking her hand in his own instead and leaned back in the chaise. A weight seemed to settle upon him, and Agnes instantly regretted adding to that burden, questioning his motives, his plan...

"We need to find Hyacinth and learn Nushka's secrets."

Her heart felt as though it had stopped dead in her chest.

"The High Witch?" she rasped. "Are you insane?!"

She couldn't believe what she was hearing. The High Witch of all immortals. Nushka's right hand.

"Nushka's blood flows through her. It is why she is so powerful. If anyone knows how to turn an army of souls into soldiers, it will be her.

And if she doesn't know how to do that, at the very least we need her to return the powers of the other Deities."

Agnes blinked once, twice, taking in his words. She rose to her feet and began pacing the room, a million thoughts and feelings overwhelming her.

Thorn materialized before her, pulling her into an embrace and cradling her head against his chest. She hadn't even noticed him leave the chaise. His steady breaths and the thrum of his heart soothed something deep within her. She inhaled his scent, which reminded her of the oak forests back in Alearia, entwined with a smokey undertone. She suddenly felt tiny and insignificant. She counted herself foolish for daring to dream of a trouble-free eternity with Thorn.

"All will be well, my love. Deep down, I think Hyacinth is just a monster like you and I, looking for something more. She likely dreams of a better life for herself and her clan. That is what we have to offer her—what will win her to our cause. A light in the darkness, as you and I have been for each other. Together, we will change the universe. Together, we will ensure there is a place in this life and the next for all the monsters needing someone to guide them to the light."

The conviction in his tone left little room for doubt, though a part of her soul still felt unnerved by the plan. In her human life, Agnes wouldn't have cared less about placing others in harm's way if it meant achieving her own means. But drawing the peaceful souls of the Afterworld into a battle that they shouldn't have to contemplate felt like crossing a line that even she did not want to tread.

45

Shaking her head gently to stifle the fear and worry tiptoeing in, she forced some of her swagger to the surface, the mask that had treated her well in the past.

Sensing the change in her, Thorn pulled back slightly to peer into her gaze, a small smirk pulling at his lips. "Now... Where were we, Princess?"

Holy heck, that gruff, husky accent had her weak at the knees. Heat flooded her core, fire flaring in her eyes.

"I believe you were just about to show me how thoroughly you intend to ravish me for the rest of eternity," she declared, mirroring his smirk.

A low laugh escaped the God's lips. "Then I better get to work. I wouldn't want you to think my skills are lacking."

After casting her a sly look, he lifted her up into his muscled arms. Gently cradling her, he strode for the balcony off their suite. The sun kissed her skin, nothing but clouds and endless sky surrounding them.

"Perhaps I'll start by reminding you exactly how I enthralled you in my spell and how thoroughly I intend to worship you for the rest of our immortal lives."

Gods save her. Agnes's heart fluttered giddily at the thought of their first joining on a balcony not so different to this one. Her mind wandered to memories of a star-filled night, when the God of War had

carried her with a gentleness that had shattered and remade her heart ...
and now how thoroughly he intended to do it again.

The Goddess of Darkness

"As the saying goes, 'If you want something done right, you'd better do it yourself'," Lilith sighed as she gazed from the top of a rolling knoll at the dawn light reflecting off the first flurries of snow settling on the grass at her feet.

She stopped to breathe in the fresh crisp air and the woodland scents of a land she had not traversed in many, many years.

Only once since the creation of her realms had Lilith crossed the line between the mortal and immortal lands and stepped onto the soil of her subjects. On that day, she had foreseen the damage and chaos her subjects would fall prey to if the wrong ruler had been appointed to the Alearian throne. On that rare occasion, she had felt compelled to intervene, as if the cords of fate were weaving a tapestry that even she could not refuse. She had been a different Goddess back then—had invested greater consideration into the mortals' trivial day-to-day issues. Very rarely did their insignificant plights touch a nerve in her now, or stir unfamiliar feelings of compassion or pity.

The humans' daily worship had increased in recent times, as was to be expected following her sister's ascension as Queen of the Gods. That had been the first hint that Nushka's reign of terror had breached the mortal realms that had previously fallen under Lilith's domain of protection. The Goddess of Darkness tried to ignore the human pleas echoing in her soul and focus instead on her increasing strength from their praise, worship, and petitions for hope. She would tend to them later, but for now she needed to focus on the end game, reminding herself that in overthrowing Nushka she would inevitably be granting their wishes for peace and protection.

With perfect posture, hair of darkest night and her voluminous shadows trailing behind a gown of thick ebony velvet, she descended the hill with a grace only immortals could achieve. Bright-eyed, she took in the surroundings, embracing the unfamiliar environment and welcoming the change from her usual lackluster existence.

A silent command had her shadows descending the hill, scoping the terrain ahead of her and weaving amongst the age-old oaks as they searched for signs of her prey. Her clouded visions had revealed a Wendigast camp nearby as one of Hyacinth's recent locations, but whatever veils the High Witch or Nushka had placed upon her meant she had been unable to pinpoint the exact location. Regardless, it would not take her long to locate the High Witch and her Clan—not now that she was in such close proximity. Her shadows were able to scope large distances. On clouds of darkest night, her shadows detected traces of burning herbs and spells, followed by the scent of spilled blood as they continued searching. Following the trail of breadcrumbs, Lilith and her shadows explored the forest's depths, slowly winding towards a town she could now see smoldering in the distance.

✢

Lilith could hear their cackles and cheers of glory long before she spotted the first of the witches. It was hard to miss the ancients whose power radiated off their traditional bark-plated gowns, their spindly spider-silk hair floating in the breeze. A small group of gangly witchlings raided the few remaining buildings in the quaint, isolated village. Others sated their appetites, both physically and otherwise, from the small group of young men entrapped with vine bindings, formed from their elemental giftings. Clever, wicked creatures, hidden from humankind for so long, now evidently left unchecked and granted full permission by their Dark Goddess to roam and wreak havoc as they wished.

Where Lilith traversed on the outskirts of town observing her prey, the river ran red with the blood of discarded human remains. Gore caked many of the witches' mouths, worn like a badge of honor. High and lost to the frenzy of bloodlust from glutting themselves upon the mortals, they did not notice the Goddess in their presence. Her sheer power simmered beneath the surface, her shadows concealing most of her features from view.

Up ahead, the darkness whispered to her of the prey she sought, the immortal she needed to enlist to her side. She would not reveal her hand or her desperation for aid. No, Hyacinth, who was honed from Nushka's blood, would only respect power. Intimidation and fear were the only languages the High Witch would understand, and she planned to use those two weapons to their full potential in the coming hours.

Stalking through the giant pine trees' shadows where the snow formed a soft blanket upon the ground, Lilith drew closer towards the

High Witch, her power calling to her like a rich wine. A shield of darkness clinging to her body prevented the wet, cold mush from seeping through her shoes. Lilith forgot how much she truly detested snow, pretty as it was.

Unfurling her shadows as she edged around the remains of a charred produce store, Lilith left the shield of the tree line and crossed the expanse of the town square. The High Witch's entourage eyed her curiously, but cautiously as they noticed the powerful clouds of darkness pooling at her feet. Hyacinth, however, knowing exactly who she was, assumed a fighting stance. Lilith's power was like a beacon to mortals and immortals alike. Revealing herself to the witches in her true form and releasing the dampener on her power was an irresistible summons to the witch clan. Power always called to power.

"What are you doing here?" the High Witch hissed. "You are not welcome, Lilith." At the mention of her name, the other witches grew wide-eyed and retreated a step.

'Cowards,' Lilith thought to herself, stepping closer.

"Such a pleasure as always, Hyacinth," the Goddess purred.

With a wicked smirk she unleashed herself, sending waves of her shadow magic towards the witches. Vines as thick as chains ascended from the ground in self-defense, but their elemental manipulation was useless against the Goddess's magic. She sent her power flooding down the airways of half the High Witch's sentinels, causing them to collapse in a heap on the sodden ground. The remaining coven members she restrained with her shadows, binding them with ropes of darkness that constricted their bodies further with every futile attempt to squirm and free themselves. Screams of fury and terror filled the air. More and more witches flowed into the square, their attempts to attack the Goddess rebounding against the impenetrable shields of night erected to protect her.

Lilith couldn't help the squeal of glee that escaped her lips as she unleashed her magic so freely. The power so often built within to near suffocating levels, and this demonstration of her power released the pent-up tension she had been holding for far too long.

"Enough!" Hyacinth screamed across the cacophony of noise. "Enough Lilith! You have made your point!"

A slow, wicked smile spread across the Goddess's lips as she recalled her shadows. The sky cleared and, along with it, the sight of the carnage unleashed, revealing more than a dozen witches lying face down in the mushy snow. Another dozen or so grunted and squirmed, fighting at the bonds of darkness holding them firmly to the ground. The remaining witches, Hyacinth included, sneered at her, shields of vines erected before them. The air was taut. An opaque shield of night was all that separated the Goddess from the witches' vengeance.

"Let us start afresh," Lilith drawled. "You know that your power is no match for me."

Hyacinth straightened, towering to her full height, her gangly fingers clenched at her sides. "Why are you here, Lilith?"

"You will address me as *Goddess*. You must remember your place, after all. I wouldn't want to have to report this blatant disrespect to my sister."

"If the Dark Queen and you are on such good terms, then do tell, *Goddess*," Hyacinth spat. "Why have you invaded my territory and attacked my clan without provocation?"

Lilith raised an eyebrow, then surveyed the gathered clan with as much distain and incredulity as she could summon before setting her gaze once more upon the High Witch. "We need to talk," she said flatly.

Hyacinth tilted her head, her emerald eyes simmering with rage. "I have nothing to say to you. Now release my witches from your bindings and leave before I summon the Queen and see what she has to say about your mistreatment of my sisters."

A clench of Lilith's right hand had the bound witches writhing in pain, their screams filling the air. Several witches ran to their sisters' aid, fruitlessly wrenching at their binds. Lilith's magic zapped their veins where their gangly clawed fingers met her magic, and they, too, fell to the ground, convulsing in pain as if electrocuted. The remaining witches stilled, too afraid to draw the Goddess's ire.

A snarl escaped Hyacinth. "Stop!" she screamed, bearing her jagged teeth—the same rage-filled sneer as her creator.

Nushka and Hyacinth were two sides of the same coin. Not for the first time, Lilith wondered just how much strength and power

Nushka had imbued into Hyacinth through her blood. The thought sent a shiver down her spine.

Lilith withdrew her shadows and the bound witches slumped to the ground, the screaming quieting to subdued sobs of relief and pain. Tears fell freely down the cheeks of many. Hunger for vengeance burned in the eyes of the rest.

"Now," Lilith stated matter-of-factly, "you and I have business to discuss. In private."

A flare of power radiated from Hyacinth, her gaze smoldering, though she leashed her temper. Lilith assumed it was only to avoid causing her sisters more pain.

"As you wish," she conceded through gritted teeth.

Lilith conjured a cloud of her darkness and weaved through the witches' bodies scattered along the ground, calming the darkness begging for release once more. Knowing that an impenetrable shield of darkness guarded her back was the only reason she meandered so carefree amongst the scorned sisterhood. Stopping short of Hyacinth, she raised her voice so that all in the square could hear.

"I am sure I don't need to tell you what will happen if any of you summon my sister while your High Witch and I take a little trip? This display of shadow power was a mere taste of what I can do, so be warned. Do not betray me, you answer to me now."

A deafening silence filled the air, making the Goddess smile wickedly.

"Very good," she murmured, satisfied she had made her point. "I am glad we all understand each other. Now, Hyacinth, let us go talk like civilized immortals. I have a deal for you and your coven that's too good to refuse," she said, erecting a portal of darkness by her side. With a flourish of her hand, she gestured for the High Witch to step within.

Hyacinth surveyed her witches then met Lilith's gaze. "If anything happens to my coven while I am gone, I swear on the Dark Queen herself that I will make you pay," she warned. Her spindly, spider-filled hair flared with the power oozing out of her.

Lilith's feline smile was anything but comforting. "Of course, High Witch. I wouldn't have it any other way. After you."

Nostrils flaring, Hyacinth lowered her fierce gaze and stepped from the mortal land of forest and snow into the Land of Milk and Honey, Lilith a step behind her. The Goddess sent a last wicked smile of warning directed at the clan before she disappeared, the portal closing behind her.

Anastasia

The Alearian Queen and King fought side by side, guarding each other's back. A tornado of shadow magic warped around them, protecting them momentarily from the enemy closing in. A moment to catch their breath. Cimmeris wouldn't be able to keep it up for long, his gifting strength was beginning to deplete. Expending even this small amount of power was likely a waste, but Anastasia knew he could sense her wavering strength—knew the frivolous expenditure of the shield was for her benefit more than his.

Anastasia slumped her shoulders, chest heaving, the fire lining her sword spluttered out as she conserved every ounce of energy for what little time they had left. She had long ago discarded her wolf form, afraid that she wouldn't have strength enough to return to her human form. If she was to die, she was determined to do so in her human body.

She felt at peace with the decision she had made to sacrifice it all for her family. Tash had known for many days now that the battle was nearing its end. Few gifted men and women were left holding the lines by their sides. More legionaries than she could count had perished, either burned alive by the peuchens' fire, impaled on the sharp tails, or beheaded by the jaws of the chimera.

With only moments left until Cimmeris's shield would fall, the enemy thrashing at it from all sides, Anastasia turned to face her husband.

"My love," she said breathlessly into his ear as she wrapped her arm around his waist. "It's time. You need to run. Save yourself, save our children, live. I need to know that you are all safe before I make my final stand."

The shield wavered, but Cimmeris turned in her arm, leaving his shield to defend his back. He dipped his head to press his brow to her own.

"I will not leave you. It is you and I, until the end of time. Nothing shall tear us apart."

Anastasia met his gaze, tears she could no longer hold back spilling from her eyes. Embracing her husband, she pressed a kiss to his lips that was both a promise and a goodbye. As their lips parted, devastation filled his golden brown eyes.

"Do not ask this of me, Tash. You are all that I have. You know I cannot leave you," he choked out. "I won't."

Anastasia's lip quivered. "I will live on through my daughters and sons. They must survive to carry on our legacy. They are the future of a better world. But I cannot leave my people to perish. You know that I will fight until my very last breath defending those who cannot defend themselves. You *must* go. Use your shadow magic and evacuate with the children. Don't stop moving until you find somewhere safe, even if you must flee to the ends of the world. Keep my children safe."

Cimmeris lifted her chin and cupped her cheek with such tenderness, wiping away her tears. He kissed her with the same ferocity as the shield that separated them from this life and the next. She committed the passion to memory, and it was that intensity that made the tightness in the Queen's chest ease.

He pulled away for the last time. "I will see you again my love. In this life or the next. We will be together again," he promised with such heartbreaking conviction.

"We will my darling," she promised, offering him a small smile, though she could not stop the tears falling. "Please tell our children that I love them with all my heart and that I will always be with them. I love you."

"I love you too," he whispered as he pressed a kiss to her forehead and shadow walked her within the temporary safety of the internal battlement stairwell.

After pressing another devastatingly brief kiss to her lips, he shadow walked away in a blur of darkness to where Anastasia hoped her children were still safely hidden. His immediate absence left her cold and empty, and a gaping hole tore open within her, as if a part of her had left with him. She fell to her knees clutching her chest, her sword clattering to the muddy stone stair beneath her. Heaving great sobs, she pulled her knees up to her chest and leaned against the wall, her heart in pieces from the knowledge that she would never see her children again. The grief threatened to destroy her from the inside out. A moment later, in a blur of shadows her sister materialized by her side.

"Tash?" Alecia spoke with a sincerity that surprised the young Queen. Anastasia lifted her head, and the same crystal blue eyes of their mother met her own watery gaze. Alecia slouched down on the stair beside her and pulled her close.

"Did you send him away?" she asked without judgement.

Anastasia took several deep breaths, trying desperately to pull herself together and suppress the sobbing gulps that had overcome her. As she spoke, her shoulders shuddered, her whole-body trembling.

"I couldn't bear to lose him Alecia. Not after all I have already lost. One of us needs to live and Cimmeris is the only hope our children have of surviving. I needed to protect them... Does that make me a bad person?" Her thoughts were so raw, she could only admit them to her sister, who had been her trusted confidant her whole life.

Alecia looked upon her with a mixture of awe and sadness. "I think you are incredibly brave, and I would not blame you if you left with them too..." The offer in her words, the heartbreaking loyalty and love revealed in that one sentence brought Anastasia to tears once more.

"You are too good to me, Alecia. You were always the bravest amongst us. Thank you," she whispered.

Her sister gave a small nod, the echo of a smile pulling to her lips. "You are stronger than you know, Tash. You are my inspiration, and no matter what you decide, I will support you."

Anastasia pulled away from her sister's embrace and stood, picking up her discarded sword from the ground. Offering her free hand to her sister, she pulled Alecia up to stand by her side.

"Let us go out in a blaze of glory that would make Mother and Father proud. Together, we will be reunited in their loving embrace in the Land of Milk and Honey," Tash promised.

"I am with you little sis," Alecia agreed solemnly, offering her a small, reassuring smile. "We cannot go on much longer. You know what needs to be done."

Anastasia inhaled and exhaled deeply. "Agreed... It is time."

Swords blazing with renewed fire from within, the two fire wielding sisters left the safety of the stairwell and entered the raging hell of the open battlements where friend and foe battled in a devastating dance to the death.

"Retreat!" General Alecia bellowed down the battlements, frantically ringing the bell at the stairwell entrance. Other bells sounded urgently in response. "We will guard your backs!"

With that, Anastasia and Alecia erected a fiery shield of raging blue flames, pouring every drop of their giftings into this final desperate attempt to save their people and defend the walls.

Their shield poured out of them, extending farther and farther down the battlement walls, incinerating beast after beast before they had a chance to react. Holding steadfast, the sisters battled side by side, defending the soldiers as they fled behind their fiery shield and into the stairwell leading deeper into the castle.

As per the final desperate plan, Anastasia hoped and prayed to the Goddess that the remaining legionaries would be strong enough to entomb their people within the lower levels of the castle while the sisters did all they could to hold back their enemy. She prayed their sacrifice would not be in vain. If all went well, her people would be granted the freedom to choose their own ending. A small chance at life or a chance to die with dignity. That was all she could offer her people now. She prayed that, by some miracle, the children and their mothers would find a way to survive. Her heart would accept no other option, for she had failed to protect them as their Queen.

"I love you, Alecia, and I will have your back until the end," she promised.

"As I have yours," Alecia vowed.

The God of War

Thorn, lounged across one of two elegant gold filagree thrones, glass of whisky in hand, watched in amusement. Lilith emerged into the open-aired amphitheater amongst the clouds from a flurry of her own darkness, Hyacinth a step ahead of her. A single wooden chair swathed in mist at the foot of the dais awaited the High Witch's arrival. The slight flare of Lilith's eyes was the only surprise she would show at his attendance. He offered her a small salute with his glass. He wouldn't reveal all his cards, not even to his sister. A small advantage in an endless game of power, even amongst allies.

"Greetings witch," he drawled, his tone dripping with distain. "How gracious of you to join us today."

Hyacinth perched awkwardly on the chair that was entirely too small for her long torso and limbs. Being made of wood, the chair itself likely set the half-tree-spirit half-witch on edge. Perfect, although Hyacinth's sneer and jagged teeth didn't exactly comfort him either.

"I would hardly call being summoned under duress a welcome invitation," she hissed at Lilith, disregarding the God of War as though Lilith was the apex predator in this situation. Bugs crawled amongst her spindly spider-silk silver hair, not bothering the witch in the slightest.

Lilith ascended the veiled stairs to the dais, her shadows trailing behind her. She took her seat upon the throne beside Thorn, folding one leg over the other, her dress clinging to her slim figure.

"You were brought here," Lilith said, ignoring the witch's obvious discomfort, "because we have a proposition for you. And if I were you, Hyacinth, I would *listen* to what we have to say, or you will find that my sister is not the only Goddess with claws."

Hyacinth leaned forward, tempests of wind swirling around her sharp claws. "You dare to harm my coven and then expect me to be amicable towards you? I owe you nothing!"

"This is war," Thorn interrupted, drawing both Lilith and the witch's attention. "We do not have the luxury of playing nice or the time to coddle your delicate sensibilities."

A glimmer of approval shone in Lilith's eyes as she looked down her nose at their enemy's creation.

"You will find, High Witch, that it is in your best interest to hear us out or else my brother and I will have no choice but to show you what we are truly capable of if provoked," Lilith warned in a sickly sweet tone that Thorn knew would only lead to trouble.

"I am loyal to my clan and my Queen. Compared to her, you two are nothing! I will not work with you. If that is what you desire, you are wasting both of our time." Icy venom and pure distain coated every word.

Lilith sent flames of darkness, cold as ice, flaring in a ring around the High Witch's seat, inching ever so slowly towards the immortal at its center. Sweat beaded on the half-tree-spirit's brow as the show of power extorted the Wendigast's greatest fear.

Hyacinth hissed, as she leaped from her seat, withdrawing into herself. "Cease this magic before I unleash myself upon you."

The dark fire halted, but they flared in warning, setting the High Witch further on edge as she sucked in a breath.

"It has been an age since I have harmed your kind, but after you came to Nushka's aid and brought about the downfall of my kin's magic, I find myself feeling little sympathy towards your plight," Thorn assured her, knuckles white as he tightened his grip around his glass. "So, calm the fuck down or I will show you just how much I would enjoy extracting your help through other methods..."

Thorn took her silence as acceptance of her situation, and with a nod to his sister, Lilith extinguished her flames, earning a sigh of reluctant relief from their captive.

"Now, let me tell you what I need from you..." Lilith said as she leaned forward, her shadows taut as they sensed their master's fixed attention.

As Lilith detailed their plan, Hyacinth's emerald eyes narrowed as she eased back onto her wooden chair and began clacking her clawed fingers against each other. At the very least, the High Witch was now offering them the respect of listening to their outrageous suggestions without saying a word. A small win.

"This is madness," Hyacinth said with utter certainty after Lilith had finished saying her peace.

'You're not wrong...' Thorn agreed, though he wisely kept his musings to himself.

"Allies do not have to like each other to share a common goal. Whether or not you acknowledge it, we are the better choice here. The better choice for not only you, but your sisters. Side with us," he urged in his husky tone. "Work with us, and in return, we can create a better world for you and your clan."

Thorn was no stranger to negotiations, and many found his frank approach reassuring. Thorn just hoped that Hyacinth was clever enough to see his claims for what they were: the stark truth.

"After all this is over," he continued, pausing only to take a sip of his drink, "you and your coven will not be allowed to roam freely, destroying mortal lives. You will not be permitted to destroy villages and run wild as you have been these past few weeks. *But,* we will ensure there is a place for you in the mortal world where you are free to live without fear of retaliation or retribution. A place you and your clan can finally call home and, in doing so, put an end to your wanderings."

The High Witch's eyes softened slightly, but her shoulders remained stiff. "What you are asking of me is the highest form of treason towards my creator. If I betray her and you do not win this war, what will prevent her from destroying me and my kind in turn? There are things Nushka can do to our kind that are far worse than the quick death you will likely gift me if I refuse to aid your cause."

'And that's the real question. If this all went to the fucking Pitts, can I keep my word and keep the clan safe? Likely not. But I would try, because I am a man of my word and I have never stood by and watched others suffer when they didn't deserve it.'

Thorn leaned forward in his chair, resting his arms on his knees. Fierce emerald eyes met his own determined gaze. "My word is my honor, and I swear that if you help us, I will treat you with the same dignity and rights as any other under my protection. When my own kin were suffering and attempting to flee during the battle, I did all I could to protect their backs as they fled for safety. I promise to do no less for you and yours."

A warm breeze drifted into the amphitheater as Hyacinth leaned back in her chair and considered his words.

Lilith levitated from her throne and descended the stairs, her shadows playing gleefully over the cloudy floor. The Goddess retracted her shadows back into herself, revealing her full lithe figure, dressed in one of the elegant onyx gowns she favored that fit her thin frame like a glove. The Goddess offered her hand to the High Witch, a gesture Thorn had never witnessed her make before.

With the offer outstretched, Lilith lowered her head to meet the witch's gaze. "Our history may be marred in conflict, but our goals remain the same; a better world for all. Work with us, Hyacinth, and together will make it happen."

Hyacinth eyed the Goddess suspiciously, but reluctantly outstretched her own clawed fingers and took the Goddess's hand in her own.

"Let your actions speak louder than your words, Gods," the witch warned. "I will agree to work with you, but only if you prove that you truly mean to treat me and my sisters as equals. I need to see how you intend to make real allowances for my kind in your new world."

Lilith offered a small nod. "I couldn't agree more. But know this, witch, if you betray us, I will wipe you and your kind from existence."

A flicker of amusement crossed the witch's face. "Likewise," she agreed, extending her claws just enough that they dug into the Goddess's skin, drawing tiny droplets of icor. The Goddess sent a jolt of her darkness at the witch in reciprocation.

A thrill shuddered through Thorn. The witch had literal claws and she wasn't afraid to use them. The three of them would get along just fine. Lilith released Hyacinth's hand and turned her unshielded back on the witch to meet Thorn's gaze—the first sign of trust she would offer Hyacinth.

"We are done here. I trust that you can show our guest to her chambers and provide her with all that she needs to carry out her task?"

A glimmer of mischievous delight shone in his eyes as he met Hyacinth's gaze again. "It would be my pleasure, High Witch."

"Good," Lilith said. "I have business to attend to."

With a flourish of her hand, a portal appeared before her. To where, he did not know, but she disappeared through it without a trace, leaving the pair of newly-allied immortals behind.

Abandoning his glass of whisky, Thorn rose from his throne and sauntered down the stairs. With an unnecessarily firm grip, he grasped the witch's gangly wrist, preparing to shadow walk her back to their palace amongst the clouds, but not before he slyly added with a wink, "It's time to play nice, *Witchy.*"

"Likewise, *God.*"

The Goddess of Darkness

It had been five brief years since the Hall of Souls had been so cramped. So many souls, taken too early due to the devastation of war. The battle of Alearia felt like it had only been yesterday to the ageless Goddess. Time had long ago lost meaning, as each day merged into the next. Being back in this place, this... prison, had the Goddess on edge.

In the beginning, her realm had felt like a haven of sorts. Though, as her long-lived life unfolded, the peace began to feel like isolation and the solitude became suffocating. A realm deprived of love or physical contact. A hell realm of its own. But for all the hurtful emotions being back in *her* realm triggered, it was still a relief to feel anything. Even the familiar sterile atmosphere of this place felt mildly comforting.

So many years spent fulfilling the same role of Guardian of the Gates—the judge of all eternal fates—had felt monotonous, making way for the gaping hole of numbness that took hold of her heart. Empathy, compassion, love, were all emotions that had been erased from her mental memory as she desperately sought to grasp any true feeling beyond hopelessness.

The thousands of frightened souls awaiting her judgment had not been brought to her doorstep because of a trivial mortal battle. The smell of trauma and fear filled the space. The Pitts had transcended the mortal land, and none were safe. The same Kingdoms' peoples she had watched over and protected all these years, receiving their prayers and her renewed strength in exchange, were now little more than an endangered species.

If Lilith and her brother did not act soon, within a year the mortal race would be eradicated and there would be no one left to restore the Gods' strength through their praise. All would be powerless but for Nushka and Thorn. Like rich wine, Nushka drank in immortal and mortal fear alike, and, with each day she reigned, her powers only grew. Battle and conflict brought Thorn renewed strength with each beseeched prayer and clash of a sword. However, when the battle was over and there was no one left to fight he, too, would be doomed. His only hope was to turn Nushka's dark army against her and draw strength from their own internal conflict.

Unless humanity was saved, Lilith was acutely aware she would lose her gifts. The thought sent a chill down her spine. Before the ball that had brought about the downfall of the Gods, such a thought had been inconceivable and utterly laughable. Now, it was a harsh reality and soon she would be no better off than the Gods trapped, powerless, in The Pitts. Nushka had utterly fucked them all, and she knew it.

Thankfully, with a hall cramped with souls begging for compassion and forgiveness, Lilith felt her strength surge to its former glory. A soft aura now radiated from the Goddess's pores. Her shadows danced eagerly around her feet with renewed vigor. For the first time,

Lilith considered delaying their judgement, extending their desperate pleas just a little longer...

Mentally backhanding herself and shaking the horrible thought from her head, Lilith gracefully descended the shrouded stairs from her throne of bones. The wails of the bone-entrapped souls were drowned out by the suffering of the souls awaiting judgment. As Lilith approached the first trembling soul awaiting their ruling, she tilted her head, predatorily surveying the male before her with her bright emerald gaze.

"Hand," she commanded, generously offering her own palm for the young solider to grasp.

A jolt of electricity zinged through their veins at the physical connection as the Goddess opened the doorway to her gifting and projected it upon the poor soul before her. Lilith sifted through the young gentleman's mind with her gift of discernment like a book still awaiting its final chapter to be written. Solomon, the dark-haired, short-statured man's name was. She had heard it whispered in his memories in the loving embrace of his wife whilst they made love on their wedding night. A pious family, who had raised their children to dutifully fear and worship their Goddess.

"Very good," Lilith murmured, the young man's grip easing ever so slightly in response.

His last memory of his family was of his young wife attempting to hush their three young girls, who barely reached his hip in height. The young ladies clung to his legs, begging their father not to leave them.

Frightened for their own sake as much as their father's. Their mournful cries could be heard long down the road after their father had departed.

Two horses were saddled up that day. One had taken him to join his comrades for battle, and the other was for his family to flee to the next Kingdom in search of safety. Setting out with barely enough provisions to last the week-long journey, Solomon still clung to the desperate hope that they had made it to Quillencia safely. Little did he know that The Pitts had invaded all the mortal realms and no Kingdom was safe. It was likely that his wife and children would soon grace her hall within the coming days if they hadn't already. She snatched back her hand. An unfamiliar feeling began to stir in her stomach.

Lilith stumbled back a step. *I caused this... It is my fault that the halls are full. It is my fault that Nushka is free from The Pitts... Would they beseech me with their prayers if they knew the truth? If they knew the role I have played in their demise?'*

"Please, Goddess," Solomon begged, voice shaking as he dropped to his knees and pulled desperately at the hem of her gown. "Please forgive me for my sins and return me to my family so that I may protect them. They are all I have. I am no one without them!"

Lilith's chest tightened. Tears welled in the man's eyes, unable to spill from his soul's new form.

"I cannot return you to them," she whispered, biting her lip.

Hopelessness filled the man's gaze and he dropped to the floor, slamming a transparent fist into the ground fruitlessly, howling from grief. Lilith took a steadying deep breath and lowered herself to kneel before him. She had never bowed before anyone, and the hall went silent at her action.

"Do not fear," she whispered, lifting his chin ever so slightly to meet her gaze, desperately wanting to ease his pain. "You will be reunited." Her voice quivered.

A spark of hope shone in his eyes. With another deep breath, she suppressed the nausea churning in her stomach.

"In the Afterworld, you will all be free of suffering. You will be safe, and you will see your wife and three beautiful daughters again."

A pained sob escaped the soul. Hopelessness devoured the man's eyes, but with a sense of dejected acceptance, he nodded his head, the movement barely perceptible. The Goddess knew she could do no more for him. She rose and offered the man her hand once more, her shadows pulled back to reveal her porcelain skin.

Through the Gate to the Afterworld, the Deity and solider walked together. A place of healing and hope awaited Solomon on the other side.

"Thank you, Goddess," he whispered softly at her back as she turned and disappeared back through the gate, leaving him to his eternal resting place.

It was by the entrance, likely pacing restlessly upon a plane of clouds, that he would await his family's arrival, unable to find any peace or move on until he knew they were safely by his side. Lilith only hoped that, once they were reunited, they could help each other heal from the heavy sorrow and heartbreak that would surely weigh upon their shoulders.

Solomon's story was not isolated. It was one of many that Lilith was doomed to sift through countless times that afternoon in the Hall of Souls. The weight of their grief and despair extended to loved ones doomed to follow their demise. The room was stifling, as though there wasn't enough air in the realm. For the first time in a very long time, she felt deep sorrow for her subjects and for those that had loved and lost so much.

After reading the minds of departed soul after departed soul, the hours trailing on, the Goddess soon realized that, despite the war raging in the mortal lands, uniting many of the humans in the fight against evil, not all souls were as pure and well-intentioned as Solomon's. Many had sought to profit from the war or used it as an excuse to commit unforgivable crimes. It was those miserable excuses for mortals that made the Goddess's blood boil and who found themselves sentenced to an eternity in The Pitts. It was a fate Lilith would not wish upon her enemies, but a fate that was nonetheless appropriate for those she deemed beyond redemption. As far as Lilith was concerned, those wretched souls deserved all that Nushka's monsters had in store for them.

Despite Nushka's dark armies' current wave of destruction wreaking havoc upon mortal and immortal realms alike, Lilith reflected that even if the battle against her sister was won, The Pitts of Moor and Nushka's unique form of punishment would still have a necessary place in the Afterlife. The scum she sentenced to the dark realm belonged nowhere else and she would never allow such souls to destroy the peace of the Afterworld.

The Goddess of Darkness

With a heavy sigh, Lilith summoned a bottle of wine to her hand and opened a portal, the Hall of Souls almost empty. Even now, as she readied to leave, more victims of Nushka's dark army began refilling the hall at the base of her dais. It would not be long before the hall grew overcrowded again.

'They can wait for now, there will always be more souls to judge. A never-ending gift—or curse—for me to deal with upon each mortal's demise... For now, it is time my sister and I had a long overdue chat. It is time for my next move in this endless fight for power.'

She straightened, her shadows skimming the hem of her gown and her chin held high as she sauntered through the portal from the safety and comfort of her realm and into the enemy's den.

The sun had long since set. At the sound of the Goddess's heels clicking against the cloud-shrouded marble floor of her chambers, Nushka turned from her lounge upon the suite balcony and snarled. Her harem of handmaidens momentarily paused their ministrations. The stifling humidity was the first thing Lilith noticed. The raging electrical storm on the horizon, was the next.

"I see you have yet to overcome the weather issues. Perhaps removing the God of Season's powers was a little hasty," she remarked, shrugging her shoulders as she approached her sister's chamber.

Aside from the flashes of lightning, several hundred floating candles illuminated the space, casting a soft glow of romantic light around the bedroom, so at odds with the beast who ruled the realm. The smell of sex and wine filled the air.

"Lilith," Nushka groaned, flexing her claws. "To what do I owe this unwanted interruption?"

With a heavy sigh, the Queen rolled her shoulders, arching her back as she lounged back upon the chaise. The silken material of her gown rippled as the handmaiden went back to work beneath their master's skirt. Lilith tilted her head slightly, brow furrowed momentarily when it became evident her sister had no intention of dismissing her servant.

"I bring a peace offering," Lilith offered, lifting the bottle in her hand.

Summoning two goblets from a cloud of darkness, she filled them to the brim. This bottle of red wine was one of the oldest in her collection. Lilith had been saving it for a special occasion that had seemingly never come, and with the realms literally falling apart around them, now seemed as good a time as any to break out the good wine.

On a cloud of darkness, Lilith sent the first glass to her sister, who snatched it up, drinking deeply. She took the second glass in her own hand and discarded the now empty bottle on a nearby table. A soft moan escaped her lips at the first sip. The wine tasted just as opulent as she had hoped. The Goddess of Darkness savored the smooth, rich wine as it passed her lips, allowing the aphrodisiac ingredients in the wine to melt away the tension in her shoulders.

"I don't know about you," Lilith sighed, her shadows floating off her back like a gently cascading stream, "but it's been a particularly hard day and I need a distraction and a drink. A squabble with you seems like a fitting end to a mind-fucking disaster of a day."

Nushka huffed a laugh, reclining in her chair and resting her eyes.

"Well, sister, as much as I would love nothing less than to indulge your pitiful tales of woe, as you can see, I'm busy." Nushka peeped open her eyes only long enough to take another sip from the glass she had been gifted. "Please show yourself out."

Lilith raised her brow and smirked. "I can see I have caught you at a bad time, but before I go, I need to know just one thing…"

Nushka's nostrils flared, and she glared in her sister's direction. Her piercing gaze levelled Lilith. "Spit it out, Lilith, then leave."

Lilith scoffed, taking a seat on the adjacent chaise to the Queen, stretching her legs out before her, making herself at home. The chair felt like a cloud, the soft velvet fabric somehow not sticking to her skin despite the heat.

"I have always wondered how you do it, you know," Lilith feigned interest, taking another sip of her glass.

Nushka closed her eyes once more. "You don't take a hint, do you?" she groaned.

With a thrust of her free hand, Nushka pushed down upon the servant's head hiding beneath her gown and pushed her away. The handmaiden slinked out from beneath the hem of her master's dress, licking her lips before a flourish of Nushka's hand had her returning to her spirit form.

"What is it you are dying to know?" Nushka asked eyeing her up and down.

Lilith conjured another bottle of the rich, rare wine and poured herself another glass before setting the bottle on the table beside her. Eyeing the retreating handmaiden with curiosity before taking another long sip of her wine, Lilith redirected her attention back upon her sister, enjoying every moment of inconvenience she caused her.

"I'd much rather a male beneath me," she said absentmindedly, shrugging her shoulders. "Though it has been far too long... So, I can see the appeal of both. At least a woman would need less training. It doesn't hurt that your handmaidens are always easy on the eye." Lilith flashed a conspiratorial grin.

Nushka scoffed and straightened upon her chaise, refilling her own goblet with more wine from the table at her side. "That they are," she conceded, offering her a salute of her glass, which Lilith echoed in return. With another flourish of her clawed fingers, Nushka's fanning handmaidens dropped their fronds and retreated to the shadows. "So, what do you want to know?"

"I want an escape," Lilith sighed, resting an arm behind her head, her shadows exploring the room. "I want to fuck someone until I ache and fall in a heap of sweat and satisfaction. I want to feel like a Goddess again."

Nushka leaned forward. "Do you have someone in mind?" she asked curiously, taking another sip from her glass.

A cool breeze drifted in from the oncoming storm, a welcome reprieve from the intense humidity.

"Well, there aren't exactly any options available to me in the Afterworld are there? The Gods are in The Pitts, excluding our brother, of course." She tilted her head back, surveying the few stars peeking through the cloudy night sky. "So, with no other options available to me, my question is, how do you do it? How do you make a soul whole again so you can fuck them like there's no tomorrow?" She downed the last of her glass, a pleasant heart radiating through her as the wine began to take hold of her senses.

Nushka licked her lips as her eyes lit up. "That, sister, I could help you with, but it would be far more fun to show you…"

With a snap of her fingers, four male souls appeared before them. Their soldiers' uniforms, thankfully clean and in pristine condition, adorned them. Another flourish of the Goddess's clawed hand had the gentlemen stripped down to their drawers, startling Lilith. Nushka's serpentine hair swayed frantically around her as she beckoned one of the straight-backed, self-assured souls before her with a curled finger. The soul's eyes flashed in anticipation and recognition as he approached the Queen and knelt hungrily before her as if this was not the first time he had been summoned.

Nushka cupped a clawed hand under his chin, her heated gaze meeting his own.

"Just as Father imbued the first gifted mortals with the essence of the Gods, gifting them with a trace of our blood, all you need is a spark of energy," she explained. "Think of it like a ball of light, a catalyst of your power."

Nushka abandoned her glass and grasped his other hand with her own, drawing it to her chest where he began teasing and palming at her breast in his spirit form.

"Just a speck of your life force imbued into a soul is enough to return them to corporeal beings. Visualize your life essence flowing from deep within into the soul you want to reanimate and cut the thread of energy once it has taken hold." she said.

The temperature in the room momentarily flared as Nushka worked her magic into the gentleman before her. The spirit worshiping her returned to his physical form a moment later, her body growing taut beneath the thin, delicate fabric as the Queen could finally fully appreciate his handiwork. A soft hiss of pleasure escaped her as his other hand met her thigh and trailed inwards through a slit in her gown, inching higher and higher as the Queen's gaze grew voracious.

Another snap of Nushka's fingers had the remaining three souls returned to their corporeal forms. On silent feet, another joined the first soldier and knelt by the Queen's side, his fingers drawing aside the neck of her gown and drawing her breast into his mouth.

Lilith turned away as she clenched her thighs together. She discarded her glass, readying to leave, but the remaining two souls approached her, blocking her way. Heat flared in their gazes, devious grins on their faces. Lilith watched as a bead of sweat trickled down one of their lower abdominal muscles, quickening her beating heart.

"Stay," Nushka commanded, but kept her gaze fixated on the soldiers worshiping every inch of her wraith-like figure. "There is enough to go around for the both of us."

Another moan escaped Nushka's lips as the first soul removed his last item of clothing, pushing the second male out the way and straddling the Queen possessively, the back of her chair lowering on a phantom wind.

Lilith averted her gaze back to the two gentlemen before her. One offered her his outstretched hand.

"Let us take you somewhere a little more private, Goddess, where we can worship every inch of you just as you deserve," he promised. His deep, gravely tone had her clenching together, heat pooling within as desperate need and impulsivity overwhelmed her senses. An all-consuming desire to feel wanted, worshipped, and whole again overcame her.

'Perhaps I consumed a little more of the wine than was wise...' she conceded, but shoved aside the thought, allowing the wine to cloud her better judgement.

Lilith let the man lead her deeper into Nushka's suite, the sheer curtains and crisp white sheets of the enormous four-poster-bed already drawn back by the other soldier. The pungent scents of aftershave and musk flooded over her—smells she had not encountered in what felt like a lifetime.

With whisper-soft touches, the soldiers pulled upon the silk knots of fabric that tied the gown over her shoulders. The unfamiliar feeling of touch amplified the urgency flooding the Goddess's core. Her form-fitting gown fell in a pool of night at her feet, lost amongst her trailing shadows. Her matching ebony bone corset and lacey under garments vanished in a cloud of smoke, replaced by the shadows that clung to her like a second skin, tickling and tingling every sensitive part of her. A calming breath had the shadows pulling back, revealing her delicate porcelain skin beneath. Her guests drank in their fill of her with ravenous gazes.

The Goddess allowed them to lead her up the last steps to the bed, one of the men taking her into his arms and lowing her gently upon the bed's crips linen. In tandem, the men worshipped every inch of her, tending to the Goddess of Darkness's every desperate desire, drawing sounds from her that she hadn't made in a century. Desires she hadn't had the courage to voice were satisfied, as if the beings before her were availed of every dark fantasy that had ever graced her dreams.

They drank from her, sucking and teasing her wetness until she could no longer take it and pounced upon the man closest to her. Her skin shone like a newly formed star as their worship of her body renewed her strength. His length pummeled into her with each rise and fall of her hips, and all the while his fingers massaged the bundle of sensitive nerves that had her screaming. He continued thrusting into her as she unleashed herself upon him. Hard and fast, they met each other's desperate call. From behind, the remaining solider wrapped his arms around Lilith and began taunting and teasing her breasts, all the while sucking at her ear lobes and neck, sending electricity surging through her core.

A breathy scream escaped her as she found her release. Now on her back, the first soldier explored her with his tongue, fingers pummeling within her, drawing out her orgasm. The second bent over her, sucking at her breast, massaging the other with his free hand. The Goddess fisted his dark scruffy hair, bucking into the other's mouth as he explored and teased her.

A wave of ecstasy overcame her, the feeling so potent it replaced the day's despair with an inconceivable amount of contentment. She abandoned all sense of control and danced beneath the sheets with the men long into the night, exploring and tasting every inch of each other. As they drew out each other's pleasure, her own soul felt as though it were shattered into a million pieces.

"Universe help me, I could get used to this," she moaned breathlessly.

In a home that was no longer a haven. In a bed that was not her own. On a night where every overwhelming need had been sated, Lilith was given the keys to the Kingdom on a wave of unending pleasure. She had learned all she needed to know and all she'd needed was her very best wine.

Agnes

Each step felt arduous, the weight of guilt pressing down upon her shoulders making each step feel harder than the last. Agnes knew she had been avoiding this conversation for far too long, but the time had come to face her demons and reconcile with her past. She doubted she would ever fully move forward without doing so. Since her arrival in the Afterworld, she had not stepped a foot out of the castle in the clouds, afraid that one misstep would mean she'd be captured by one of Nushka's creatures and returned to The Pitts. She pictured her former mistress laughing at the mockery of hope Agnes had built in her heart of the possibility of being able to live out an eternity in peace. That day had yet to come, and Agnes thanked the Goddess of Darkness and her beloved for that.

"What do you see?" Thorn asked softly.

Agnes looked up—truly looked and took it all in.

Her heart stopped in her chest. It was just as she remembered it, and yet it wasn't. She recalled Thorn once telling her the story of the Afterworld and how it had been created to morph into whatever the soul seeking refuge had desired. The same general elements existed, but how they appeared was unique to each soul, reflecting whatever their heart needed most to attain peace.

Agnes dropped to her knees. The cloud-shrouded ground of moments ago now felt like soft, plush grass. The scent of pine drifted by on an early winter's breeze, the first snow of the season sticking to the ground. She carefully picked up a clump and tasted it; cold, icy water coated her tongue. Dark brown eyes drew wide in awe as Agnes let the remaining snow fall to the ground. She rose to her feet and wrapped her hands around Thorn's waist. She buried her head against his firm chest, the tears she could no longer hold back beginning to flow.

Thorn wrapped an arm around her, drawing her closer, stroking her hair with the other. Muffled sniffles filled the otherwise quiet realm, the seemingly impossible sound of birds chirping in the distance the only other sound.

"Are you well, my love?"

The tenderness of his question only had her crying more, a flood of emotions consuming her.

"It's just like I remember; the snow, the mountains, and, there—" she whispered in between sobs as she pulled out of his embrace, pointing to the tallest alpine peaks of the mountain before them. "It looks just like Castle Brandistone, just like home, but it can't be..." Brow furrowed, she shook her head in disbelief as she bit her lip.

"Why can't it be?" Thorn pressed, taking her hands in his own, looking down at her with sympathy and compassion radiating through his gaze.

"Because it isn't real. My home is back in the human world," she explained, shoulders slumping, tears once more welling in her eyes that she blinked away.

Thorn offered her a small, understanding smile. "It is as real as any other realm, my love."

He moved to stand by her side and wrapped an arm around her. Together they looked up the mountain towards where she had pointed. Agnes wondered what the castle looked like to him.

"The Land of Milk and Honey is a place of healing and a place of hope," he claimed, pulling her in closer. "Though it appears differently to each soul seeking refuge, their experience is no less real or important. All souls grieve in their own way, and the Afterworld provides what they need to heal. Often, that place is their mortal homes—their place of refuge from the troubles of the former world. There is comfort in familiarity, and I hope that this realm provides that for you, regardless of your newfound immortality."

He turned to meet her gaze and pressed a hand over her beating heart. "*You* are my home," he said, his voice wavering. Thorn's sandy blond hair ruffled in the gentle breeze. "Wherever you are is where I want to be."

He pressed a soft kiss to her lips. His scent wrapped around her heart, intermingling with the familiar woodsy-pine smell of Alearia. She committed the moment to her memory.

"If your heart desires to replicate the Kingdom of Alearia," he continued sincerely, "if that is where you most feel safe, then that is where we shall make our home in the Afterworld."

Agnes's heart clenched and she felt her knees wobble.

"You are too good for me, Thorn. I do not deserve you."

As soon as the words had escaped her mouth, she was struck by the honesty of them. Thorn looked upon her with pity in his gaze as he shook his head in dismay.

"I am unworthy of you, Thorn," she whispered, a tear trickling down her cheek.

Biting her lip, she dropped her gaze and pulled away from his touch, needing to place distance between them, the vulnerability revealed in her words almost too much to bear.

Thorn grasped her hand before she could walk away.

"Don't run, Agnes. I know what we share is new, but I have been waiting a lifetime to find someone who makes me feel the way that you do. Now that I have found you, I'm not letting you go. I will decide what I can and cannot handle. And you, my love, are all I will ever want, in this life and for all eternity."

He stole her breath away as he pulled her once more into his loving embrace and kissed her until her lips felt swollen and she became breathless. The sense of urgency in his touch made her heart clench. For all the wretched things she had done in her past life, she couldn't fathom how the universe had rewarded her with the God in her arms. For, as long as they had, even if by some blessed miracle they had all of eternity together, she would never stop feeling unworthy of having his whole heart. She would thank the universe every Gods damned day that he looked at her as if she were the only thing that mattered—as if they were the only two immortals in the whole universe and damned be the rest.

"Are you ready?" Thorn gently asked her, drawing her from her thoughts.

Agnes took a deep, steadying breath, willing her heart to calm and the fear threatening to unravel her to subside.

"Will they be there?" she asked, gesturing towards the sandstone castle upon the mountain top. The towering building glistening in the sunlight reflected off the freshly fallen snow.

Thorn gazed back upon the horizon. "Your family will be together, wherever their souls feel most at peace. So, yes... I think your family home is as good a place as any to start looking," he said, offering her a small smile which she reluctantly returned. Her heart rate began pounding once more in her chest.

"I'll be here by your side, every step of the way," he promised, giving one of her hands a small, reassuring squeeze.

Agnes took another deep breath and grimaced. "Then you'd better prepare yourself for a shit show. I guess it's time for you to officially meet my parents."

The laugh that bellowed from Thorn made her grateful all over again that she, of all people, could call him hers. Together, they began to make their way across the snow-shrouded valley towards the castle perched amongst the mountain peaks. Each step felt a little heavier than the one before. No matter what was about to unfold, she would be grateful to have Thorn there by her side. Agnes only hoped that once he saw who she truly was through her family's eyes, he would not run from her blackhearted soul. She wondered if their newfound love would survive the test.

The God of War

Standing at the base of the steps leading to Castle Brandistone's main gates—or at least the Afterworld's version of the Alearian castle gates—Thorn wondered if what was revealed to him was the same as what was projected to his lover. A great burden weighed upon her. He saw it in the way she trudged up the mountainside and in the shadows that marred her gaze.

Thorn knew she had done many terrible things in her mortal life. After all, only the worst souls were sentenced to The Pitts of Moor. But he had done the same. You cannot be the God of War without having tipped the scales unforgivably in one direction or another, always unsure if you had chosen the right side... if there were ever a right or wrong side to begin with. His actions had meant the rise and fall of Kingdoms; in comparison, nothing she could have ever done would compare in his eyes.

He knew there was more to Agnes's story, and he wasn't naïve to think otherwise. Villains were not born evil, just as the heroes in stories are not without blemishes. Many shades of grey mar a person's soul. People were not simply good or evil as far as Thorn was concerned, and the more he grew to know the spirited woman that held his heart, the more he struggled to see her in any other light than a lost girl trying to make peace with her past and find her way back home. He hoped that, despite all that was about to unfold, today was the first step in her journey to finding peace.

The gates to the castle groaned open with a thrust of Thorn's elemental magic, and he led the way inside, clenching her hand reassuringly lest she fear he would run at the first sign of trouble. He was here to stay. He only hoped they lived together long enough for her to believe it.

A pathway had been cleared from the gates to the castle. The sound of horses baying in their stalls could be heard as they passed a stable on their left. The cobblestone pathway looked worn from the thousands of people who had graced the castle. The fine details in the vision before them were likely replicated perfectly from Agnes's memory of her former home. Even the unfamiliar smell of pine caressed his senses. A smell he had not encountered since watching the battle of Alearia unfold five years earlier.

An unfamiliar feeling rolled in his stomach as he remembered that, at that time, despite the chaos that had befallen the Kingdom, his beloved had been dealing with much worse as a handmaiden in The Pitts of Moor. Thorn kicked a loose pebble, rolling his shoulders and stretching his neck as they continued to walk. The urge to defend her was almost too much to resist.

"Are you ready for this?" he asked softly, as much to himself as his partner, the sound of his question mostly drowned out by their footsteps shuffling on the cobblestones.

Straight-backed and head held high, Agnes walked confidently, as if drawing upon an old defense mechanism.

"I have no choice but to be ready.".

He offered her hand another gentle squeeze as they stopped on the doorstep. Unsure of the protocols for unwanted guests in the Afterlife, Thorn struck the door knocker three times, and they waited in silence.

"All will be well, my love," he said with a small smile. "I am here for you."

Several moments later, the carved wooden door to the sandstone castle creaked open, revealing a vast hall with the banners of House Brandistone and House Caston lining the walls. Candles like the ones used in the Land of the Gods floated near the ceiling, illuminating the space. Before them stood a stern-faced gentleman in his fifties. He wore the military regalia of a seasoned warrior, adorned with service medals, and a gold filagree crown with red rubies perched upon his head. The semi-transparent soul took in Thorn's imposing stature, his muscular tattooed arm, shoulder-length hair and facial hair with cool detachment, his nostril flaring as his gaze moved to settle upon the woman at his side.

"How dare you come here?" King Titian Brandistone sneered, arms crossed in front of his puffed-up chest. "We have worked hard to rebuild after your betrayal. Your unwanted presence will unravel all the healing your mother and sisters have made. Leave now. You are not welcome here."

Agnes took a step back just as four female spirits, accompanied by a young adolescent male spirit, came into view by the former King's side. The oldest—likely his wife--took his hand in her own. Two young women dressed in amour adopted protective stances by their parents' sides, one crowned with a simple diadem that could be attached to a helmet if needed. The other sibling—a healer, judging by her soft aura and clothing—stood back, allowing the others to take the lead. The younger male took a step closer to the crowned armored woman's side. So, this was Agnes's family, whole once more, but not in the way they should have been. An entire family robbed of the long lives they deserved.

"Good afternoon, Your Highnesses," he offered gently. "I am Thorn, the God of War. Welcome to my domain."

His voice caught a little on the last word, his accent thick, as was generally the case when his nerves crept in. He questioned, given the hostility radiating from the family before him, if referring to his Deity status at such an occasion had only made matters worse.

King Titian gulped a useless breath and bowed his head.

"Welcome, God of War. Please forgive my temper. There are many issues left unsettled between the woman at your side and this family. Though, that raises the question: may I ask why this wretched outcast is in your company?"

Agnes's hot-tempered mirror, the rigid King looked down his nose at his daughter as if she were the Queen of The Pitts herself, sent to doom them all. What could have made someone hate her with such ferocity, Thorn did not know.

"Perhaps I underestimated the difficulty of this anticipated meeting, Agnes," Thorn remarked in jest, offering a small laugh that was not reciprocated by the royals.

"With all due respect, God, this is no joking matter," Titian seethed, a vein pulsing in his semi-transparent temple.

"That traitor nearly brought about the downfall of my Kingdom," Titian raged. "She murdered her own mother for God's sake! She deserves to spend eternity in The Pitts for all she has done."

Thorn took a step forward, his temper rising with every disrespectful word that belittled his lover. "Know your place," Thorn said in a low voice. "I do not take kindly to such disrespect towards the ones I love."

Agnes's gaze flicked from her father's to Thorn's as she dropped to her knees. "It's all true," she confessed, breathing raggedly. "I am a monster, and I deserve nothing more than the fate Lilith sentenced me to." Her voice quivered, as if she feared Thorn would love her any less now that the demons of her past were laid bare before him.

He looked at Agnes as though he were seeing her for the first time. They had never delved deeply into her past. He only knew the basics of her crimes thanks to a briefing with his father prior to their first meeting.

"I always knew there had to be a good reason that you were sentenced to The Pitts," he admitted, and Agnes dropped her gaze, tears spilling freely from her eyes. "But having served Nushka in such a degrading, soul-shredding way for so many years means you have served your penance and more. If I could, I would erase all the soul-destroying memories of your time there. You have earned your right to forgiveness, Agnes."

Agnes looked at him through tear-filled eyes, biting her lip.

"Despite all you have done in your past life," Thorn continued, "I promise that I will make my sister pay for every moment you were under her control. That fight will be a battle worthy of song."

Agnes sobbed through a small huff of laughter. "I would like front row seats to that," she grimaced, earning a full belly laugh from Thorn.

He looked upon the woman who had breathed purpose back into his long-lived life, ignoring the rising tension in the room—radiating particularly from her father. He smiled softly at his beloved. "There is nothing you could ever do, or have done, that would make me love you any less," he vowed to her.

Agnes's smile lit up her eyes. A rare moment he would remember for as long as the stars permitted him. She turned away from him, biting her lip as she stared longingly at each member of her family, lingering on her stern-faced father who Thorn was inclined to flatten for looking at her with such disdain. Rolling his shoulders and reining in his anger for the wretched soul before him, Thorn redirected his attention back to Agnes.

Her sorrowful gaze rested upon a young woman with a much less extravagant crown atop her head, the battle-worn amour she wore in her final moments amongst the living still adorning her body as if she had only recently arrived in the Afterworld. The woman likely still clung to hope of rejoining the mortal world.

"Anastasia," Agnes breathed, her eyes shimmering. "How did you come to be here?"

Thorn placed a supportive hand on her upper back as she knelt before her family. Anastasia looked with haunted, grief-stricken eyes towards her sister.

"I had hoped you were him," Anastasia whispered, her voice cracking. "I thought you were Cimmeris. I had clung to the hope that he and our children would be the next to arrive," she sobbed, voice trembling as her body shook.

Agnes drew a hand to her mouth, her breath catching.

"I don't know what kind of a mother that makes me," her sister admitted, "to hope to see them again and know that it would only come if they, too, had left the land of the living."

She took a step back, shuffling on her feet, unable to hold Agnes's gaze any longer.

"I miss them so much," she explained, blinking back the tears, voice quivering. "They are my whole heart, my family, and I want nothing more than to return to them and protect them. I miss them more than I can even explain, and I will find no peace until we are united or I know they are safe..."

She took another step back, Agnes's face dropping at the sight, the weight of her role in the war likely weighing upon her shoulders as heavily as it did upon his.

"I'm sorry, Agnes, but I can't do this," Anastasia stated abruptly, shaking her head. "I can't listen to whatever apology you planned for all the hurt you have caused me and our family in the past. I believed in you when no one else did. I freed you so that you could have a chance to start over somewhere else, and in return you kidnapped and tortured me. You left me in a cold storeroom to lie chained in my own filth. How could I ever forgive you for that?"

Thorn exhaled deeply, taking in her words as the crimes of his lover continued to be listed off. But he did not let her words affect him. What was done, was done. The past was the past. There were many things he also wished he could change about his own past, but could not. He knew the feeling of shame that no doubt threatened to consume Agnes, and he wished he could relieve her of that crushing burden.

"I'm sorry, but I need to go," Anastasia continued. "I have more important things to worry about than dredging up the demons of our past."

Her sister turned on her heels and, with impossibly heavy steps despite her spirit form, started to walk away.

"Wait!" Agnes called, rising to her feet and reaching to grasp her by the arm, but the sentiment was lost when her hand ran straight through the transparent soul of her sister.

Anastasia stared back at her, tears welling in her eyes that could not spill.

"Please!" Agnes begged, her high-pitched pleas conveying her desperation. "Just hear me out. I know I can't take back what I have done. I can't return you to your family, but please hear us out. I'm trying to make amends for all the harm I have caused."

Agnes's chest was heaving now as she tried and failed to calm herself.

Her voice cracked. "Please!" She bit her lip, but backed up a step to grant her sister the space she needed.

"We need your help to save not just your family or Alearia, but all humankind." Her final words seemed to strike a chord with Anastasia, who met Agnes's gaze cautiously.

Anastasia dropped her head, her body trembling.

"I gave my life to give my family a chance to survive, and I failed them," Anastasia said softly. "There is nothing else I can do for them now." Her voice cracked at the admission that must have broken her heart to share.

Thorn stepped forward to stand by Agnes's side, taking her hand in his own and squeezing it. A mixture of grief, sorrow and anger lined her family's faces. The older woman, who stood faithfully by her King's side, stepped forward and released her husband's hand.

Silver wove amongst the same honey blonde hair as her daughters. A crown matching Anastasia's graced her head, marking her as the former Queen of Alearia. Wrinkles around her mouth and eyes revealed the joyous life she had led, and the soft blue eyes revealing great loss and strength surveyed him in turn.

"I am Amealiana, the former Queen of Alearia, and before you are my whole heart, my family." She bowed her head low before him. "May I introduce my son, Alexander, taken far too young by the woman at your side." She sent a reproachful glare directed at Agnes before indicating the two women who looked strikingly alike. "Annie and Anastasia, my twins, and my joy. Alecia, my strong-hearted defender, and lastly, my husband, who you have met. Not all our lives were lost at the hands of my daughter, but if it were not for her, I might not be here today, and perhaps neither would the rest of my family. One ripple can start a chain reaction. I don't know what I did to fail her so badly and cause her to hate us so much, but it is Agnes who was the downfall of this family." She spoke forlornly, unable to meet her daughter's gaze.

Thorn gripped Agnes's hand even tighter, desperately wishing there was a way he could ease the pain he knew she was going through, her hand trembling in his own.

"But," Amealiana continued reluctantly, "she is my daughter, and I will always have a place for her in my heart. Devastating as her actions were, I know deep down that she is someone worth saving, as it appears you can attest to, God." She smiled softly.

Thorn nodded his head in understanding. "We all make mistakes, some more horrifying than others. I cannot speak for Agnes, but I know that I have done many things in my life that I wish I could take back. All any of us can do is spend each day trying to be a better person than we were the day before."

Deep, soulful brown eyes met his gaze as Agnes smiled softly, making Thorn's heart clench.

"We hope to set things right," he continued, directing his full attention to each of Agnes's family in turn. "We have a plan to bring an end to Nushka's dark army and cease the invasion threatening not only your living family, but all families in all the Kingdoms. But we cannot save them alone. We need your help."

"Not just your help," Agnes added with as much confidence as she could likely muster in the face of those she had hurt, "but the help of all the spirits with warrior hearts in the Afterworld."

Titian stepped forward, his posture rigid and his face stern as he wrapped a protective arm around his wife's side.

"Leave us out of it," he declared, meeting both Agnes's and Thorns gaze. "We have lost too much already, and we will not be pawns in whatever game you have planned. You will not put my family's eternity at risk."

Thorn felt his temper start to rise again, but Agnes's reassuring squeeze of his hand helped him to calm down before he said something he would regret. But it was Anastasia that stepped forward and interrupted his train of thought.

"Will this plan save my family?" she asked cautiously, her spirit shimmering in and out of focus as her form shook.

"We hope so, Tash," Agnes responded gently, hand still trembling within his.

"Don't call her that," Alecia spat, staring daggers at her sister. "You lost any right to call her that the day that you betrayed her." She stepped to her sister's side and took Anastasia's hand supportively in her own, the Afterworld making touch from spirit to spirit possible.

Agnes flinched, but ignored the barb and instead placed her free hand over her heart. "Even if you decide not to help, I promise I will do everything in my power to save your family from Nushka's reign of terror."

Anastasia cautiously surveyed Agnes before nodding shallowly, a small peace offering.

"I will be honest with you," Thorn interrupted, all eyes now on him. "The army we are up against brought about the downfall of my kin and the Land of the Gods."

He thought it wise to leave out his own role in the hostile takeover. It didn't seem wise to add further fuel to the fire. "It will take an army equally as invincible to stand a chance against it," he warned.

Anastasia eyed him suspiciously. "What good could a realm of departed spirits play in this war? A war you say even Gods could not win?"

Sensing the tides beginning to change, Thorn pounced on the opportunity and offered the warrior heart a conspiratorial grin.

"The odds may be stacked against us, it is true," he declared matter-of-factly. "But together, we are going to raise an army of the dead to save the living. And you and I," he nodded towards her, "are going to lead it."

13

Anastasia

"An army of the dead…" Anastasia pondered, the thought taking hold in her mind. "That is all I am now… Someone whose life no longer counts amongst the living. A spirit with no purpose, a mother with no children… and now, apparently, a Commander to an army of spirits which, unless I have completely lost my mind, is impossible."

"Don't let him get in your head, Anastasia. False hope is all this so-called God of War offers you. He doesn't care who he hurts, spreading his lies," King Titian said, stepping forward and wrapping an arm around his wife's side. "With all due respect, *God*, you've lost your mind! I suppose that is not unfathomable for someone so long-lived. It's even more likely, given you have fallen in love with *Agnes*, of all people. Perhaps we should be concerned about your mental state."

"Love surely is blind," Alecia quipped smugly, crossing her arms, her stance more relaxed now.

The God of war stiffened, but refrained from biting back, instead focusing his attention on Anastasia as he awaited her response. She bit the inside of her cheek, one brow raised as she appraised the pair before her.

If it were possible now, Anastasia knew her heart would be racing. In her human life, it would have felt as though there wasn't enough air in the realm to sate her lungs. But she wasn't that teenage girl anymore. She had grown and learned to conquer her fears and anxiety. She had learned to breathe through the onslaught of emotions. She was the master of her feelings now, not the other way around. Except now, everything had changed. The air she breathed did not sustain her—the action itself was pointless. Her heart no longer beat, little more than a phantom sensation in her chest.

"I had always thought that, with death, so would come peace," she at last voiced, ignoring her father's barbs at the God. She had never appreciated distasteful jokes about mental health, especially when she had such a complicated history battling her own inner demons. "It brought me solace to think of my loved ones finding eternal peace in the Land of Milk and Honey. But the Afterlife is not so black and white. There are too many words left unsaid, too much I still wished to accomplish. Too many hopes and dreams torn away from me with a slash of one serpent dragon's barbed tail."

She took a deep, pointless breath and Amealiana started rubbing her back reassuringly.

"I was barely into my twenties," she continued, though her voice trembled. "A devoted mother to multiple children, a loving wife, and until yesterday, the Queen of Alearia. I cannot comprehend how, after my heart had only just begun to feel whole again, that my life could be so irrevocably torn to shreds," she trailed off.

Her hand trembled as she gripped Alecia's palm tighter in her own, seeking the reassurance of touch to ground her, trying desperately to shake the anger and despair clouding her mind.

"It is okay to be afraid, Tash," Alecia whispered in her ear. "You have loved and lost so much. Our spirits exist in a land that looks like our home, yet it is not. The world smells just like home, and yet it doesn't, as if the illusion tried and failed to live up to reality. A poor imitation of the real thing, missing the vital people who matter the most to you."

Her crystal blue eyes met the understanding gaze of her elder sister, as if she had read all the thoughts straight from her mind.

"It's disorientating, isn't it?" Anastasia replied.

Alecia smiled knowingly. "I don't think I'll ever get used to the stables smelling so good," she joked, drawing a chuckle from the remaining family.

The God's shoulders appeared to relax ever so slightly, seemingly grateful for a moment of laughter to relieve the growing tension in the room. A slight upturn of her lip was all Anastasia could manage.

"A century or more without my family, seems like its own kind of torture and I'm not sure if I can bear it…"

"I know, Tash, I know…" Alecia replied sympathetically.

Anastasia knew her elder sister was trying her best to be helpful and supportive, but Alecia could never fully understand how deep her grief ran or how much she wished she could bargain anything in exchange for just one more day with them. Even the loss of their parents was hardly comparable to the well of grief now pooling in Tash's stomach. Especially now that they had been reunited in the Afterlife.

'A small part of me hopes that the war is lost, so we will be reunited...' she thought desperately but did not dare voice that selfish thought out loud.

Anastasia pulled her hand out of Alecia's grasp and moved to perch upon one of the velvet wing-backed chairs in the entrance way.

"I want my children to live happy, long, full lives, even if I can't be a part of it," she declared, a glimpse of the Queen she had been shining through. "If there is a way to at least save those I love from meeting the same premature fate, then it is worth exploring."

She surveyed her family who returned her gaze, offering small, reassuring smiles. Anastasia's eyes suddenly widened, blinking several times as she finally took in Agnes's appearance. Her useless heart caught in her chest as she tore her gaze from Agnes to take in the God of War's similar, softly glowing appearance. He shone much bright than her sister, but the glow was there all the same. Her cheeks were rosy and filled with *life...* As she peered back at her eldest sister, she sucked in a useless breath, the cogs in her mind ticking over.

Agnes tilted her head, raising a brow. "Are you alright, Anastasia?" she asked uncertainly, making to move towards her but pulling up short, deciding at the last moment to give her space. The God of War's brow furrowed beside her.

Anastasia raked her gaze over Agnes from head to toe, taking in the soft glow of her skin, the way her chest rose and fell with each breath as if she needed the oxygen. But she was in the Afterworld...

She looked at Alecia's semi-transparent skin, her expression indicating she would love nothing more than to throttle Agnes for taking a step towards her. Her family remained in spirit form around her, now watching her with a mixture of curiosity and concern.

"Are you alright, Tash?" her twin sister Annie asked softly. She was a calming, welcome presence as always. Her hand stretched out to take her hand in her own. The phantom feeling filled Anastasia's useless heart with warmth.

Shoving aside thoughts of Thorn's proclamation and her family's concern, she stared at Agnes.

"I killed you myself! How are you alive?!" she demanded to know, raising her voice.

King Titian's eyes flared, a grin spreading across his face at the news of who had brought about Agnes's death. They had not discussed it since Anastasia had arrived in the Afterworld. Titian had passed into the Afterworld before Agnes's passing, or so they had been led to believe. Anastasia had always quietly suspected otherwise, particularly when a curious owl had accompanied her on her journey to Shadows Peak as she sought an alliance before the battle to Alearia.

Anastasia had questioned his death again, during the battle of Alearia, when a giant wolf had fought by her side on several occasions.

The same wolf had sadly died at her side during the battle, having dived behind her and taken a sword to his chest that was aimed for her back. She had never voiced her doubts over his death to anyone before and made a note to question her shape-shifting father about it on a more private occasion. Now, though, his quirked eyebrow, puffed chest and proud grin revealed exactly what her thought of his daughter's actions.

Agnes chewed her lip. "You did kill me," her sister admitted, looking for support from the God beside her who offered her a small nod. "Afterwards, I was sentenced to The Pitts of Moor for my crimes."

Anastasia tilted her head as she pulled out of her twin's grip to cross her arms, trying to solve the missing piece of the puzzle. Suddenly uncrossing her legs and bolting upright, her eyes widened once more.

"It's possible!" Anastasia blurted. "You!" She pointed at the God, who now looked at her as if she were a lost puppy in need of coddling. She chose to ignore that observation, practically beaming with anticipation.

"Me?" he asked cautiously, crossing his arms and pursing his lips.

"You can bring me back to life! You're a God, you can take me back to my family, right? You did it for her, you can do it for me." The opportunity was so ripe she was internally kicking herself for not thinking of it earlier.

The God of War took a step forward, his gaze softening, arms relaxing at his sides. The thought of him taking pity on her made her blood boil.

"Don't look at me like I've lost my mind," she declared, voice wavering. "You did it for *her*," she emphasized, glaring at Agnes. "You can do it for me. That's my price!"

She stood from her perch on the chair, fists clenched at her sides. "I'll help you lead the army," she offered, "but after the battle is won, you will reunite me with my family in Alearia. You can do it! You can make me human again, I know you can! Agnes is living and breathing, and she died, so it's possible," she rambled, all hope hanging by a thread.

The God exhaled deeply. "I'm sorry, but I can't," he breathed. Those few words caused her heart to ache. "Your life's thread has been cut; it cannot be returned."

Confusion filled her as hope slipped from her grasp. "What do you mean?" she demanded. "You did it for Agnes, why can you not do the same for me? What makes her so special?!"

Agnes flinched, but Anastasia shoved aside the guilt from causing her sister pain—even if they were not on good terms. The God of War's ire met her gaze.

"Agnes was granted the gift of immortality by my sister in exchange for a favor. I do not know if it is something I can replicate. But even if I could..." his features softened as he regained control of his temper. "Your life has come to an end. Your fate has been fulfilled. It would upset the balance of the universe to return you to your family. I'm sorry, but I cannot help you."

He turned to meet Agnes's gaze, taking her hand again in his own. "Truth be told, whilst we are being completely open and honest," he paused, taking a breath. "If Nushka falls, I am not sure her gift will hold..."

Agnes's breath caught. "What do you mean? You said we would have eternity together."

Thorn pulled her close. "We will, my love," he whispered, resting his chin atop her head, wrapping his arms around her. "Nothing can separate us, no matter which form you wear. If necessary, we will reanimate you after you have returned to your spirit form, but you will not need to breathe, and your heart will serve no purpose. You will be corporeal, but not alive. You will not be able to conceive a child..." he added gently. His husky tone reminded Anastasia of the warriors from the Kingdom of Stanthorpe, his accent growing thicker as his emotions rose.

Tears welled in her sister's eyes, and a heavy pit of sorrow for not only herself began to weigh her down.

"It does not matter, my love," Thorn continued, raising his chin with a small smile, but still holding her to his chest. "I loved you before you were immortal, and I would love you no less if you were a spirit. Nothing can tear us apart in the Afterworld. You will still have me, always."

A small sob escaped Agnes as she buried her head in his chest, her arms wrapped around him tightly. Anastasia's chest clenched. Cimmeris had stared at her with a similar longing gaze. Only yesterday, they had fought back-to-back, the last hope for their family and Kingdom. Only yesterday she had held and kissed her husband goodbye, knowing that she would likely never see him again. A well of despair yawned wide within her. At least she knew her sacrifice had not been in vain. He and her children were still alive. If they hadn't escaped, they would be by her side already.

Thorn released Agnes from his embrace and turned to face her family, his gaze filled with sorrow.

"I am sorry for all that you have been through," he promised. "Losing the love of your life and being separated from your children is an unfathomable loss for anyone to bear. If I could, I would return you to your family, if for no other reason than to help heal your heart after all you have suffered."

Anastasia slouched as she took a moment to gather herself, her shoulders relaxing ever so slightly.

The God of War raised his chin and took a deep breath—a warrior preparing for battle. "I cannot give you back your life, but I can offer you a chance to help me save your family. They still need you to fight for them, even though you have already given so much," he said. "I can reanimate you and any souls who choose to fight with us, to defend the defenseless against my sister and her dark army."

Anastasia bit her lip before taking a steadying breath, the muscle memory of the action bringing her calm even if it physically served no purpose. A mixture of emotions flooded her. The brief glimmer of hope she had felt was gone, replaced with the knowledge that, even though she could not be with her family, she could still care for them as a mother and a wife. For them, she would hear what the God of War had to say. For her family, she would do whatever she could to ensure their survival.

"No love is stronger than the love a mother has for her children," she whispered.

Thorn nodded knowingly, offering her a small smile. Anastasia looked around at her family, eyeing each one in turn. Understanding filled their eyes as they each offered her a small, sorrowful smile in return.

"I have never had to fight alone, and it will not be any different this time," she spoke assuredly, her family nodding in return. That thought brought her comfort and, having already paid the almighty price, she had nothing left to lose.

She turned to face the God of War, offering him another small, uncertain smile. Shoulders back, she declared: "For my family still living, and with the help of my loved ones beside me, I will help you lead your army. Together, we will do all we can to make sure that no others suffer the same fate as mine."

Thorn met her determined gaze and offered her a shallow nod.

"It would be my honor to fight by your side," he replied, turning his gaze from Anastasia to Alecia's steely eyes, who met his gaze with a stern nod.

"Commanders," he spoke with an air of authority that filled even Anastasia with a sense of self-confidence. "Despite all odds, it's time to rally an army like no other. The dead must rise to save the living."

Agnes

Agnes descended the mountain with the God who, despite everything he'd learned of her past, still chose to stand by her side.

'I have found someone who cares for me and believes in me more than I believe in myself. Despite it all, I have found someone who loves me regardless of my failings.'

Sensing her lost in thought, Thorn paused beside Agnes and took her into his arms, pressing a soft kiss to her lips.

"How are you feeling?" he asked, pulling his head back to meet her gaze, concern etched across his features.

Agnes bit her lip and shook her head ever so slightly. "I still cannot believe you are here, choosing *me.*"

Thorn smiled knowingly, his crystal blue eyes alight. "I know exactly what you mean. Never in all my years would I have anticipated finding my match. It was a dream I had long given up on." He shrugged, his tousled hair swaying slightly in the breeze.

Agnes lifted onto her toes and kissed him, desperately craving closeness, afraid that if she blinked, he would regret his feelings for her and teleport away, leaving her alone. Thorn opened his mouth to her, deepening their kiss, rubbing a hand up and down her back as he held her. His rough stubble brushed against her soft skin.

"Gods, I don't think I could ever get enough of this," she swore. "Even if we had an eternity together, I could never get used to waking up beside you in all your glorious naked perfection. And that accent, *fuck*, that accent does things to me," she confessed unabashedly.

Thorn barked a laugh, pulling her closer, his groin pressing against her stomach, sending heat flooding through her core.

"You're not too hard on the eye either, you know?" he smirked, waggling his brows, offering her a whistle that was so human it made her smile even brighter. She playfully shoved his arm in response. After pressing his lips to hers once more, he swept her into his arms and opened a portal beside them, their suite ready and waiting for them on the other side.

"Speaking of my *naked perfection*, I think you and I have some much needed catching up to do," he suggested shamelessly.

"I couldn't agree more," she grinned as heat flooded her cheeks.

In the peace and quiet of their new home together, they made love beneath the waterfall shower, then again on their cloud-like four-poster bed. They explored each other until the sun set and long into the night afterwards, his smokey pine scent filling her soul. Despite all that lay before them—and the weight of the world on their shoulders with the battle ahead—Agnes and Thorn embraced their time together, treasuring every moment.

Agnes had always imagined that, if she were ever blessed enough to find a partner, it might take a while for her to want physical contact, given everything she'd been through in serving Nushka. But with Thorn, it had felt right from the very beginning. She always felt in control when she was with him. He made her feel comfortable and safe, never pushing her for anything beyond what she was willing to give, which, to be fair, was very little. The sex they had was fiery enough to melt and remake souls. Their soul-deep connection, something she had until now never experienced, was something she would fight for with every ounce of her newly immortal being. To Agnes, the God stretched out on the bed beside her was the answer to a wish she had never realized she'd made.

Thorn tucked her into him, wrapping an arm around her waist. Agnes breathed in the scent of him, savoring the moment, her eyelids heavy and head light. Thorn had long gone quiet, his deep breaths treading the line of sleep.

"Thank you, Thorn," Agnes whispered, needing to get the words out.

"For what?" Thorn yawned, nuzzling sleepily at her neck. She leaned further into his touch, her behind brushing against his very prominent arousal that gently nudged once more at her entrance.

She sighed blissfully. "Thank you for being there for me. For choosing me, even when all others would run," she replied breathily.

Thorn moved his hand higher up her stomach and started exploring her breasts again.

"You and I are the same, Agnes. We are both broken and healing, but beyond that, we both love beyond reason. I love you because I know what it's like to be flawed but trying your best to make amends. Our past doesn't determine our future. We are not defined by our mistakes, but by our actions in the present. You are facing your demons head-on so that we can have a chance to save those who need us most. That is incredibly selfless. I don't think you give yourself enough credit, my heart. You deserve love, Agnes. You deserve *my* love and so much more," he whispered, returning to nuzzle at her neck. His hands roved down the plane of her stomach once more, sending heat flooding through her.

"Beneath that sexy, rough demeanor, you are a such a soppy old romantic at heart," she replied through breathy giggles.

"Shhh! You are never to repeat such things again, especially not within earshot of the other Gods. You'll ruin my tough image," he scoffed, giving her a teasing squeeze.

Agnes's stomach ached as she laughed. A joyous, full sound that she could not recall making in such a long time, and it wasn't long before Thorn joined her. After finally steadying her breaths, a content smile on her face, she whispered, "I do not deserve your love, but I will thank the stars every day for it."

Thorn inched himself a little closer to her in response, pulling her in more, his firm length teasing her. Agnes's breath hitched.

He released a small sigh. "One day, I pray that you see yourself through my eyes and know that you are worthy. Until then, I will spend each fleeting free moment worshiping you like you deserve."

Pulling a hand to her chest to feel her heart race, she couldn't contain the feeling of hope that began to blossom.

"Well then, my love," she teased, wiggling a little more into his lap. "By all means, continue your worshiping."

15

Hyacinth

The *suite,* as Lilith referred to it, was unnervingly clean, the natural light far too bright and the air too crisp. The lack of grounding to the earth was unsettling. Trapped within the castle suspended amongst the clouds, the absence of greenery left her feeling on edge and detached. Whilst the luxury of amenities was a nice change from her usual life, the separation from her sisterhood left a gaping hole within her blackened heart. Whilst she detested the Bone Castle within The Pitts, its proximity unnervingly too close to the volcanic terrain, at least she had been granted the freedom to roam and sate her needs. Neither privilege was afforded to her in the Afterworld.

Hyacinth's magic hummed beneath her skin, her bark gown leaving a trail of splinters in her wake—the only mess in the otherwise pristine room. Transparent barriers surrounded the suite, maintained by the Gods' powers to keep her trapped. Despite the fine furnishings, the rooms were little more than a gilded cage, leaving her feeling claustrophobic.

Lilith entered the room through a portal of her own making, and The High Witch paused her stirring, her potion of herbs bubbling atop the fire raging in the marble fireplace.

"As you can see, I have work to do, so say your piece and kindly see yourself out."

The spiders roaming within her spindly hair stilled, as if afraid of earning the Deity's ire. Their intelligence never ceased to surprise her. Her affinity with nature and its creatures was as natural as the sun rising and setting each day.

A cruel smile spread upon Lilith's lips. Her midnight-tinted organza gown—so like something her sister would wear—stood out dramatically amongst the white furnishings. The shadows writhing around her thin shoulders and the hem of her gown flickered.

"I have come to check on your progress on the tonic to return the Gods strength," Lilith replied.

Hyacinth wondered how much further she could push the God's patience. She was in no rush to return the other Gods' powers; such an act would be of little benefit to her. Despite agreeing to the Goddess's alliance, she held little faith in Lilith's promise of a better world for the witches. As soon as the Goddess got what she wanted, Hyacinth had no doubt Lilith would dispose of her like a useless toy.

"I'm working as fast as I can," she replied, resuming her stirring, not wanting the tonic to burn.

"The Pitts of Moor has infiltrated the mortal world and, unless balance is restored soon, there will be nothing left worth saving— including your coven. After the dark army has ceased their rampage and run out of victims to taunt, they will turn on each other. Beasts are rarely content to live in peace," Lilith said, crossing her arms. "And who will you feed upon once the mortals are gone? The hearts of the young will be no more. Your power will wane without their strength and you will become as powerless as the humans you prey upon."

"Perhaps we will feast upon your powerless Kin once our Queen's war in the mortal lands is won."

Lilith's nostrils flared, sending a thrill down Hyacinth's spine. A broad, toothy grin spread across her face... she regretted it a moment later.

Darkness descended upon her, lashing at her sides, leaving slashes of pain in its wake. Hyacinth howled, but welcomed the pain, calling upon her own elemental magic, summoning a shield of air and severing the shadows' hold on her. A moment later her shield was shattered by the same shadows that lashed at her, drawing screams from deep within as she fell to her knees, completely outmatched.

Several minutes later, after Hyacinth's voice grew hoarse from screaming, the attack abruptly ended. Blinding light seared Hyacinth's vision at the withdrawal of Lilith's shadows, but her eyes re-adjusted once more to the bright, natural light of the open-aired suite. Lilith stood smugly, relishing in the lesson she had given her. A growl escaped the witch as she glared at the Goddess towering over her.

Hand staunching the black blood oozing from a particularly deep gash sustained to her gangly arm, Hyacinth rose to her feet—she knew how imposing her full height could be, even when injured.

"After I have finished this potion, then what? What is to stop you from discarding me and my kin then?"

The Goddess's features softened slightly, a little taken aback, but the fire burning within her still radiated through her aura.

"I am a Goddess of my word. I will protect you and your sisters. But I cannot do that if you do not help me restore the Gods' powers. Without them, Thorn and I will be facing a battle that will not end well for anyone."

Hyacinth's shoulders slumped and she exhaled deeply.

"To make the potion work," she sighed, "I need the scale of a peuchen, a goblet of your blood, and a member of your kin to test my potions upon. Then you shall have your remedy."

Lilith tilted her head to the side, surveying the witch, undoubtedly weighing her words with her gift of discernment. "You shall have them," she finally responded.

After one last appraising look at the High Witch, the Goddess of Darkness left the room through a portal, a gateway of light closing behind her, leaving Hyacinth behind to tend to her wounds.

The witch slumped heavily on the edge of her four-poster bed, not caring about the black ooze that leaked from her wounds onto the crisp white linen. Hyacinth placed pressure on the worst of her wounds, the bleeding slowly staunching beneath her hand. Steaming water began rising in the adjacent bathing tub. The only peace offering the Goddess of Darkness would provide her. Steam already started filling the room.

"Ut tua umbras esse maledictum.

Ut tua umbras esse maledictum.

Ut tua umbras esse maledictum."

A small curse to repay the Goddess for her newly marred skin. Now all that was left to do was wait and see if her little spell found its mark. She hoped that it struck at the most inconvenient of times.

"May your shadows be your curse, *Goddess.* It is not wise to threaten a witch," Hyacinth mused to herself wickedly. "We have teeth, and we aren't afraid to bite."

Despite the rising steam from the tub, an icy breeze rippled through the room as if in answer. Hyacinth shed her gown of plated bark, insects of all manner dispelling from within to explore the room in their master's absence. The witch limped towards the bathing area to clean her freshly clotted wounds.

Anastasia

Seated on a chaise in a replicated suite of her former home, the Goddess of Darkness imbued Anastasia with her magic. A warmth spread through her chest, radiating outwards as the power of the intimidating Deity swept through her. The tingling in her fingers was the first sign that the transformation was working. Sweat gleamed upon Lilith's brow as she poured her energy into a task that seemed much more difficult than Anastasia had anticipated. Pain seared down her arm, causing her to hiss and withdraw from the Goddess's grip. Her hand instantly returned to its former transparency.

"Son of a Centaur!" Lilith cursed, nostrils flaring and shadows whipping frantically at her fingertips.

Now that the pain was gone and the connection severed, Anastasia slumped back against the chaise. "Is there something wrong, Goddess? Thorn led us to believe that this process would be less complicated."

Apparently, she was to be the Goddess's experiment—a role she was not overly pleased about.

Lilith sighed heavily. "Nothing about what we are trying to do is simple."

Anastasia bit her lip and offered her hand back to the Goddess, trying not to fidget with the other. "Forgive me, I did not mean to offend you."

Being subjected to the Goddess's powers was the last thing she'd anticipated for the day. However, when Lilith had arrived unannounced upon her balcony an hour earlier, commanding Anastasia to make herself comfortable so she could begin her work, she was in no position to decline.

"I cannot stop worrying about my family. I need this to work. I miss them dearly and I would do anything to help them. I love them with all my heart."

Lilith tilted her hear to the side, brow furrowing.

"I have never loved in the way that you have loved," she confessed with a small shrug of her shoulders, her shadows calming slightly. "In all my years of existence, human emotions have always been a mystery to me."

She shook her head as if to clear her thoughts. Anastasia sat in bewilderment, unsure of what she had done to earn such honesty from a Deity. All the same, she was flattered and even more curious.

"A few millennia have passed since my birth at least… I lost count a very long time ago. Time is both a blessing and a curse. As it stretches on it losses its value, but it is something that you can never have enough of," Lilith mused.

"But in my long existence, Anastasia, my life has not been so blessed as you likely believe. Even though you may be parted from your love, count yourself fortunate for the time that you have shared together and the eternal existence you will have once more one day. Power and magic can do many things, but they cannot replicate unyielding love. I have seen the way Thorn has fallen for your sister, so I know love must be possible for my kind. I just haven't experienced it for myself. Maybe one day I will. It is what I envy most about humans. Without love, I feel my life will always be missing something."

Lilith leaned forward, taking Anastasia's hand again in her own, the fireplace giving off a pleasant heat that eased the tension in her shoulders. Anastasia dropped her gaze, feeling the warmth in her chest bloom and preparing herself for the pain that was sure to follow. This time, as the Goddess continued her work testing and pushing her magic, the pain that trickled through her fingers was much dimmer. Ever so gradually, to her amazement, her finger then arms morphed from tingly and transparent to a solid form.

"I treasured every moment I had with Cimmeris and my children," Anastasia said sadly, needing to fill the silence. "They are my whole heart. Every moment we are parted causes me pain so deep that I am not sure anything aside from being with them could ever make me feel whole again."

The Goddess hummed in consideration, but kept her thoughts to herself.

"Despite it all though," Anastasia pushed on, "I wouldn't change what I did. Sacrificing myself to buy my family and my people more time was the only gift I could offer them. I would do it all over again if it meant giving them a chance to survive. I suppose, in a manner of speaking, I'm going to do just that and repeat the past. But whatever I give, it will never be enough. I would destroy my soul for them and be discarded to the ether if it meant knowing they would be safe in Alearia."

Lilith said nothing. Anastasia blinked, feeling tears well in her eyes. She inhaled sharply, pulling her hand back from Lilith and holding it up before her. Tears fell freely and she sobbed, happy for perhaps the first time in her existence that she could cry.

She stared at one hand, then the other, trailing her armor-clad arms to her chest, her feet, her waist. Her body was whole once more. A sob escaped her as she leapt from the chair to stand in front of the full-length mirror, staring in awe.

"I can't believe it," she said, peering at herself in her reflection. She touched a bare hand to her face, feeling the softness of her cheek, licking her lips with her moist tongue. Real, genuine *feeling*.

"You did this!" she exclaimed, turning around, hope filling her heart as she met the Goddess's vibrant, triumphant gaze.

Lilith rose elegantly from the chaise. "You sound surprised, but it was only a matter of time. More importantly, now I know how to do it again," she grinned fiendishly, flicking her sleek, ebony hair behind her shoulders, the length disappearing amongst her living shadows.

Butterflies fluttered in Anastasia's stomach, a mixture of anticipation and apprehension fighting within her.

"What now?" Anastasia dared ask, a flood of questions rising to the surface that she tried desperately to suppress, not wanting to overstep with the Deity.

"Later today, you will summon your family and we'll repeat the process. I need to confer with my brother before I can replicate the transition. Our powers work similarly, so I imagine it will not take long for him to adapt and learn. Then after that"—Lilith smiled, a giddy wildness shining through her gaze—"we will raise an army of souls to shake the realms."

A wave of anxiety crept upon Anastasia. The shock of the unimaginable odds they were up against was finally sinking in now that reality was reflected to her in the mirror. She would see her family again and without hesitation, she would give everything to ensure their safety.

An icy breeze flooded in from the open doors leading to her balcony, causing the flames to flicker in the fireplace. On instinct, Anastasia rushed to draw closed the doors, blocking out the wind. A moment later, as she leaned her forehead against the glass door and peered outside at the flurries of snow, it dawned on her. She had never been happier to feel the crisp, icy winter breeze upon her cheeks. Anastasia knew she wasn't the same as she had been. Her heart did not beat when she pressed a hand to her chest, but the phantom sensation still lingered.

A life taken could not be restored unless under considerably rare circumstances, but for now, she embraced feeling as close to human as

140

she would ever experience again. She was eager to throw herself into battle, knowing each moment they delayed meant another that her loved ones were in danger without her protection.

Anastasia turned to where the Goddess had stood by the fireplace, but she was gone, likely having left through one of her portals while she had been momentarily distracted. The Deity was immortal, after all, and carrying the weight of the mortal Kingdoms on her shoulders. She doubted Lilith had time to waste indulging her any further

"Thank you, Lilith," she whispered to the ether. "Thank you for getting me one step closer to seeing my family."

Anastasia peered into the mirror across the room once more and stood momentarily stunned. Light radiated through her hopeful gaze, a blush of color reddened her cheeks, and the first genuine smile she had shown since arriving in the Afterlife spread.

Finally, alone, Anastasia ran to the bathing chamber. Apparently, the realm could anticipate her needs, as a steaming bath was calling her name. There were few things that calmed her nerves like the comfort of being immersed in hot water. A heavy sigh escaped her at the sight of the steaming, lavender-scented water.

An array of chocolates, a carafe full of red wine, and a fine crystal goblet appeared on a side table beside the bath, summoned on a dark wind. A gift from the Goddess before her departure, Anastasia assumed. She relished the robust smell of the wine as she poured herself a glass. Shedding her armor, mouth agape at the vision of her soft, glowing skin, Anastasia stepped into the warm embrace of the water. The hours slipped by in a blur as Anastasia spent the evening embraced within the ever-warm tub, cherishing all the pleasant sensations washing over her. The gift of touch and taste were something she would never take for granted again.

The Goddess of Darkness

Rescuing one of her kin from the dungeons in The Pitts of Moor was not Lilith's main concern. What had her on edge was the potential fallout of her actions and the possible downfall of Thorn and herself. It was the very reason Lilith had not wanted to retrieve her kin until Hyacinth's spell was fully developed. Saving them too early would mean selling herself out prematurely, leaving her with a group of powerless Gods to stand against the might of Nushka's dark army. That was a fight she currently could not win, and the thought sent a shiver down her spine.

'Until an army of the dead is raised and a cure for the Gods' conditions is concocted, I cannot risk drawing attention to myself by retrieving the Gods, no matter how terrible the conditions are in The Pitts. Retrieving just one God—a lesser God that would not be noticed as greatly, however ... well, that would be worth the risk if it meant speeding up the process of restoring their powers.'

Dressed in black fighting leathers, an array of weapons hidden within the protective suit clinging to her body like second skin, Lilith stretched her limbs, the ease of movement on this rare occasion trumping her desire to dress in her usual luxurious gowns. There was an added risk to attending Nushka's realm dressed as such. To the wrong creature in

The Pitts, her appearance could be deemed a threat, but Lilith felt confident her shadows would give the illusion that she was wearing a gown of wispy dark clouds.

Unaware of the layout of Nushka's dungeons, she teleported to the inner sanctum of the Castle of Bone. The smell of decay and smoke mingled with the smell of sulfur from the volcanoes. Lilith had only entered the Hall of Bone once and the repulsive sight was exactly as she remembered.

Upon a tattered chaise, two souls shed their clothes and fucked life rabbits. The public display of carnality left a foul taste in her mouth. Lilith was not an exhibitionist, no matter how many years she had graced the universe. A body was just a body to her, but despite the way she had witnessed her sister and other Gods live and act, she still valued having some measure of privacy when she took a lover. The events of the other night—having her urges sated by the two former soldiers, her sister only meters away on the balcony—was not an incident she cared to repeat any time soon, no matter how wild the ride had been.

"May I help you, Goddess?" asked one of the Wendigast souls, drawing Lilith from her thoughts.

"Sister," Lilith offered, turning to meet the tree-spirit's gaze, the transparency of her soul so out of sync with the memory she had of the formidable, towering witches using their elemental magic during the battle. "I have come to see the prisoners, but I am afraid I do not know the way."

The witch eyed her suspiciously. "Does the Queen know you are here?"

Lilith straightened at her incredulous tone. "I am a Goddess. Who are you to question a Deity?"

The soul took a step back. "I mean no disrespect Goddess. I merely want to know what to tell our Queen of your unanticipated visit," she added rather cleverly.

'Bitch…'

"Of course," Lilith offered, looking down her nose at the subordinate. "Tell Nushka that I've come to make sure the Deities have not forgotten her kindness in holding them captive, rather than destroying them. If I were her, I would have put their heads on spikes and burned their flesh by now, discarding them to the ether."

The witch chuckled darkly, revealing translucent, jagged fangs. Even in spirit form, her cobweb like hair seemed alive with the spirits of spiders and other insects that had previously lived within.

"In that case," she responded, wild-eyed, "let me guide you."

"As you wish," Lilith smiled softly. With a flourish of her arm, she gestured for the witch to lead the way.

They walked through the reasonably quiet Grand Hall, careful to avoid the questionable pools on the floor and the potent stench of sex and urine. In a matter of hours, when the nightly bells were rung, the servants and guests of the Dark Queen would grace the Hall for a night of depravity. Lilith needed to be out of The Pitts long before then. Thankfully, once she was shown the location of the dungeon, she would know the way for next time.

The soul led Lilith down a long, windy path of corridors and steep staircases, weaving this way and that down halls with walls made entirely of bones. Despite the rather eerie building materials, Lilith had to admit that she could appreciate the artistry in creating such a masterful structure. It was the perfect realm for such a sinister seat of power. Even her own throne of sinner's souls incased in bone paled in comparison to the grandeur of this shrine of death.

The deeper they travelled within the belly of the castle, the higher the temperature rose. Sticky perspiration clung to Lilith's skin beneath the leathers she wore. Lilith's shadows flicked agitatedly.

"I haven't the faintest idea how our Dark Queen tolerated living here all these years," Lilith mused to herself more than the witch. "Count yourself fortunate, sister, that you cannot feel the heat here as I do."

The Wendigast paused and looked over her shoulder. "We feel everything here, Goddess, especially the pain."

Lilith exhaled deeply. "I am sorry to hear that. I wish it did not have to be this way for you."

The Wendigast soul tilted her head to the side, scrutinizing her as if puzzled. Without a word, she offered her a small nod of thanks before leading the way once more.

Lilith willed her hair into a braid to cool the back of her neck. It was the first time she had arranged her hair in more than a century. The itch to reach their destination grated on her nerves, though she feigned cool indifference. Lilith already questioned if she had shown the soul a level of compassion that would draw far too much attention to her visit. News of her familiarity with the help would no doubt make its way back to her sister. The walls had ears in this place…

As they rounded another corner, the bones protruded as the staircase narrowed, the slate steps growing slick from condensation. Heat seeped through the bones that lined the volcanic rock on which the castle was built, scorching her cheeks. If it were not for her thick boots, she was sure her feet would be blistered and burnt by now.

Finally, they approached a gate of bone, darkness awaiting them on the other side. A young peuchen guard on duty blocked the entrance.

"The Goddess has come to see the prisoners," the Wendigast spirit proclaimed. Even from her towering height, the peuchen still made the witch spirit seem small.

The young creature who was many years away from reaching its full size or maturity of powers, peered down at the Goddess.

"You will need to be more ssspecific Goddess. Who have you come too sssee? We have many prisssoners here," he hissed mind-to-mind.

Lilith narrowed her eyes. "That is none of your concern. I am a Goddess and a loyal ally of your Queen. You will let me pass or I will take matters up with her."

The peuchen hissed at the threat, but tucked his wings in tighter and slithered to one side of the passageway, allowing the Goddess to move past.

"Thank you for your assistance, sister, but I will be able to find my way from here," she offered politely, dismissing her guide.

The Wendigast nodded. "As you wish, Goddess." The soul gave the peuchen a dirty look as she appraised him from head to tail, before turning back and ascending the staircase from which they had come.

Lilith tried and failed to shuffle elegantly around the peuchen, descending another dark staircase. Small intermittent sconces lit the way as she passed bone cell after bone cell. The inhabitants called out to her, attempting to grab her attention, begging to be set free of their cursed entrapment. When corporeal occupants managed to touch her, they found their limbs melted away with her darkness, the occupant screaming as a new level of pain overwhelmed them.

"Do not touch me without my consent," Lilith hissed.

The remaining cellmates drew silent, fearing the wrath of the Dark Queen's sister—a necessary role to mask her true purpose for being there.

As she ventured farther into the dungeons, encoutering the first immortal souls, likely former subjects or warriors who had failed to live up to Nushka's impossibly high standards. Then she spotted the first of the departed Gods, their souls sentenced by Nushka to spend eternity in The Pitts. She promised herself that as soon as the war was won, they would be among the first she would move to the Afterworld.

Finally, her gaze settled on a distant relative, one of the few remaining living Deities.

"Athena," she breathed, taking in the emaciated form. "What have they done to you?"

Athena and Lilith had maintained little contact with each other in recent centuries due to her long-term residence in the Hall of Shadows, but she had fond memories of growing up in the Land of the Gods with her. Lilith shook her head. The Goddess of the Hunt, now trapped underground, deprived of her powers. Lilith didn't want to imagine the torment the Goddess had been through, given her current state.

Vacant eyes met her gaze, all sense of hope drained from the Goddess who lay curled upon a bed of hay against the far wall.

"Free me," she rasped through chapped lips. Her pale, blistered skin peeked through her wafer-thin, tattered slip of a gown. Vomit and excrement lay over a third of the stone floor. Steam rose between the stones from the surrounding volcanic plains, worsening the smell.

All life was drained from Athena's eyes, the Goddess deprived of the strength to even rise from the makeshift bed. Lilith turned away, nausea welling in the pit of her stomach. "I cannot save you," she whispered to the darkness, "but I vow to come back for you and all the others, or may I deserve a fate worse than yours..."

Choosing the first God she came across would have been too obvious to the guards making their rounds. She couldn't risk it no matter how much her heart broke to see one of her own in such a broken state. Heavy-footed, she forced herself to move on.

Cell after cell offered the same sight, her people all suffering from abhorrent conditions and abuse. The Pitts of Moor was created to punish souls who were deemed too vile for a second chance. It was never meant to serve as a prison for the living. Wave after wave of guilt and anxiety washed through her at the role she had played in their downfall. If not for their immortal blood and strength, many of the Gods would have already succumbed to the unbearable conditions. Their pleas for compassion and, more unfathomably, *death*, weighed upon her shoulders worse than any guilt she had ever experienced. There weren't enough words to express her sorrow.

'How could I have been so foolish?' she cursed herself, shaking her head. Her shadows hummed beneath her skin, sending an unpleasant tingling sensation reverberating like pins and needles over every inch of her.

'How could I have let Nushka do this to our own people?'

The deeper she ventured into the dungeon, the more unbearable the conditions became. Her leathers clung unpleasantly to her already irritated skin, a headache building between her eyes.

Stopping beside a cell to her left and leaning her forehead against the bone cell bars, she tried desperately to block out the frantic pleas of her kin echoing down the dungeon hall. As death's embrace drew nearer, they clung to a false hope of freedom from the wretched hell realm. With no mortals to worship them and renew their strength, and no form of sustenance or reprieve from the terrible conditions, Lilith wondered, not for the first time, if she would be able to heal them in time with Hyacinth's tonic and free them from this hell realm.

"Lilith," a gruff male voice rasped.

On unsteady knees, Admetos, the God of Fire, crawled towards her. Lilith took a step back from the bone cell door.

"Lilith," he repeated, his face stern as he took hold of two of the bone bars. "Are you here to free us or end us?"

Lilith raised her hands before her in placation.

"I have not come to bring you harm, only to offer a glimmer of hope. I have come to tell you all not to give up. I am doing all I can to help you," she swore.

His stare could have leveled mountains, his jaw clenched as the God ground his teeth, the putrid smell of sweat radiating from his pores.

"What good is a glimmer of hope when your words mean nothing and your actions even less?"

Lilith straightened, lowering her hands. "I didn't intend for any of this to happen. It was not meant to be this way for any of us..." she trailed off.

Admetos scoffed. "Your plight must be truly dire to be able to come and go as you please. Your powers and strength were not taken from you. You have your freedom. You chose Nushka over all of us. It is only out of guilt that you are here now." He pushed off the bone door and turned away.

Lilith launched forward, grabbing his arm through the gate, his returning glare making her flinch. "Wait."

"Unhand me, Lilith, or are you taking away my right to rest as well? Have you not taken enough from me already?"

Lilith sent a wave of her cooling magic washing over him, knitting together his wounds and healing the burns on his feet. Then she summoned shoes and a new robe for him. He would still need to bathe, but that could wait.

"Let my actions speak louder than my words, Admetos," she pleaded. "Come back with me to the Afterworld. I have a plan to restore the Gods' powers and together, you can get the revenge you seek and stop the havoc raging in the mortal realms."

The God looked her up and down with disgust, taking in the clean, fighting leathers, her healthy, sleek black hair, the vigor of her shadows pulsing around her like a vibrant aura.

"You are a disgrace, Lilith," he said coldly. "After all this is over, after our powers are restored and we have sought our revenge against Nushka, after the mortals are saved and the battle is won, do not forget that we will hold you accountable for the treason you have committed against your own kin."

His back straightened. His vow and promise hit her as hard as if he had branded his words upon her skin.

Lilith's vibrant green eyes met Admetos's steely gaze. The dungeon was deathly quiet as the prisoners listened intently to their spokesman.

She held her head high. "I am still in the position of power here, despite how guilty I may feel. No matter what you think of me and my past crimes, I am your only chance at power and freedom."

The God pursed his lips, nostrils flaring. "Is that a threat Lilith? If we do not agree to forgive and forget, you will not free us?!" He shook his head. "You have not changed at all. Nushka's bitch, through and through."

He spat at her, a globule hitting her cheek. She wiped her face disgustedly with her sleeve.

"You are trying my patience, Admetos," she soothed. "I am offering you a deal, not a threat. If I prove myself loyal to you all once more, if I restore your powers, free you all and help you defeat Nushka and her dark army, *then* you will offer Thorn and I clemency when the time of judgement comes?"

"Why should I trust you?" he scoffed.

Lilith laughed darkly. "I am offering you a deal. I risk my own safety just by coming here. But the choice is yours?" She shrugged.

The God pulled out of her grasp. "I do not speak for all the Gods, as you know."

Lilith smiled, feeling the tide turning. "That is true, but you do have influence. I will free you as a sign of good faith. And, when I return for the others, they will find it is in their best interest to agree to my terms, else I fear their time will soon run out. As you know, even immortals do not do well in the dungeons of The Pitts without their strength or powers."

He narrowed his gaze at her. "Free us all now, or there is no deal."

Lilith was grateful for the bars that still separated them.

"Hyacinth is still working on the potion to restore your powers, and if I grant you all your freedom, Nushka will know what I have done and send her dark army after us. So, I need you to come with me now as Hyacinth's test subject and, once your powers are restored, I swear on my immortal life that we will return here, set the others free and restore their powers too."

The temperature rose, as if the God's trapped powers were trying to free themselves. The God ground his teeth. "Fine," he seethed, nostrils flaring. "We have a deal."

Lilith bowed her head low, concealing her smirk. As she rose, she smiled softly.

"I am glad we could reach an accord."

Offering her outstretched hand through the bone bars, Admetos reluctantly shook on the offer. As he grasped her hand, a shadow of darkness enveloped them and, through the shadows, they walked from one realm to the next. They emerged on the other side in a realm of light and peace, a restless High Witch pacing around the suite.

"Welcome to the Afterworld, Admetos," Lilith announced. "It is my pleasure to introduce your savior and my *dear friend*, Hyacinth, High Witch of the Wendigast."

The witch stopped and stared at her incredulously. "It took you long enough," Hyacinth snapped, glaring at her. "Though I am glad to hear we are suddenly on such friendly terms."

"Yes, yes," Lilith said, rolling her eyes. "I do apologize for the delay. It turns out breaking into an enemy dungeon is surprisingly easy. Convincing a God to set aside their stubborn ways and volunteer to assist you, however, was another matter," she drawled.

She turned and offered Admetos an overly sweet smile.

"Our very helpful High Witch will restore your powers. Now, if you will both excuse me, I have more important things to do than supervise this questionable experiment."

The Goddess redirected her attention back to the High Witch.

"Play nice and *please* ensure Admetos is alive and well when I return," she said, raising a brow.

Hyacinth scoffed, mumbling something that sounded awfully like a curse. Lilith exhaled deeply, rubbing her temple, feeling her ever-growing headache take a turn for the worst.

Admetos stiffened at her side. "You cannot mean to leave me alone with her?!"

Lilith paused, dropped her hand and grinned, revealing sharp teeth as she released a fragment of her shadows in a wave of frustration.

"I was under the impression that you wanted your powers restored." She smiled sweetly. "If you would like to waste more of my time, you are welcome to join me as I attempt to raise an army of the dead."

Admetos froze, mouths agape as he looked at her in alarm. Lilith sighed exasperatedly.

"A clever Goddess uses all resources at her disposal," she stated matter-of-factly. Summoning a black velvet bag, she turned and handed it to the witch. "Before I forget, here are the other ingredients you requested including a sealed jar of my blood."

Hyacinth raised a brow but nodded as she took the satchel and peeked inside. "It's all here. Thank you."

Begrudging the prospect of spending one more moment in either immortal's presence, she opened a portal and left the God and Witch to their own devices.

Hy

18

The God of War

At the foot of the stairs leading to the Afterworld's castle, stretching out to the horizon, the souls of the Afterworld stood in answer to Thorn's summons. Dressed in a gown of ivory silk, her long blonde hair plaited over her shoulder, Agnes looked like a Queen as she held his hand beside him. Seeing her dressed like this took his breath away and made him wonder what future they would have together if the fates and universe allowed it.

"You look beautiful," he whispered in her ear.

The blush that rose upon her cheeks made him smile.

"You don't look too bad yourself," she said, waggling her brows, making him laugh.

Lilith appeared through a portal at his other side, dressed for battle and, a little disheveled, to his surprise.

"Do I want to know where you've been?" he asked curiously.

Lilith glared at him. "Just a small matter of retrieving Admetos from the dungeons of Moor... Nothing to be concerned about. Unless Nushka realizes. In that case, we will need to raise the barriers *and* our army before we ruin our chances of saving the mortals and our kin."

Thorn blinked several times.

"So, just another ordinary day then?" Thorn scoffed.

Lilith barked a laugh. "Yes, brother, just another day of screwing up the universe in every way possible. However," she added, her tone grave, "this was a calculated risk. Hyacinth needed someone to test her potion on and, without a volunteer to assist her, we would be no closer to reuniting the Gods with their powers. They are a vital component in our plan."

"So, we're in the business of stealing Nushka's allies and prisoners now," he mused, squeezing Agnes's hand in reassurance. "It won't be long before she discovers we are double crossing her. Perhaps the next time you commit another crime against our sister, you could let me know first?"

Lilith rolled her shoulders. "As you wish," she sighed. "Forgive me, Thorn, but after spending an eternity in the Hall of Shadows, I am used to working alone. The idea of consulting others is new to me."

He nodded, offering her a smile as he appraised her knowingly. "We both have much to learn, but I have no doubt that you did what you had to."

Turning back to the souls restlessly awaiting their formal address, he nodded to Anastasia and her family—now reanimated thanks to his efforts earlier—and they ascended the stairs to join their group. They needed to present a united front if they were to gain the volunteers needed to boost their army.

Thorn rolled his shoulders, preparing himself for a different kind of battle. Diplomacy was unfamiliar to him, but inspiring speeches were not. He released Agnes's hand and gave her a not-so-subtle squeeze on her ass, chuckling softly to himself at the way her cheeks reddened. He took several steps forward, chin held high.

"Welcome. My sister, The Goddess of Darkness, my partner, Agnes, her family and I, would like to thank you for answering our call. It is my honor to speak to you all today."

Thorn bowed to the souls of the departed, who bowed low in a wave of solidarity in return. The gesture moved him—it was not often that he garnered respect off the battlefield. Lilith stepped forward to his side, her shadows stirring at her feet, intermingling with the soft clouds that covered their steps. Her appearance still surprised him. He couldn't remember the last time he had seen her in pants.

"Greetings, my subjects," Lilith began. "In the short time since taking over our sister Kiara's seat of power, we have ruled over this realm with kindness and compassion, ensuring that your afterlives offer the peaceful eternity that you all deserve. However, as many of you may know, the mortal realm and the realms of the Afterlife are in strife."

She turned to him, offering Thorn a nod of affirmation to continue, having both agreed in advance that it made more sense for him to take the lead in this instance. He just hoped their plan went well. Some of the souls towards the back, unaware of how far the Gods' vision stretched, murmured amongst each other.

162

"All Kingdoms are in grave danger, as the mortal world is no longer protected from other realms. Our sister, Nushka, The Goddess of Blood and Bone, has taken control of The Land of the Gods. She has crowned herself Queen and entrapped our remaining kin. As I speak, her dark army of creatures continues to wreak havoc upon the mortal realms," he declared.

The stench of fear and anxiety filled the air. He took another step forward.

"But all is not lost," he assured them, his voice carrying upon the power of his wind to the far reaches of the assembled crowd. "We have a plan to restore peace and to save your families."

The atmosphere changed, the weight of fear mingling with apprehension and confusion now written across the souls' faces.

"The Goddess of Darkness and I will protect you. We will not allow your afterlives to be disturbed. Very soon, we will lock down the realm. No one, not even Nushka herself, will be able to penetrate our barriers and enter without our permission," he declared.

That reassurance seemed to ease some tension as many of the crowd relaxed their tense shoulders, the quiet chattering amongst each other less hurried.

"We cannot save the mortal realms alone. We need your help." He kept his tone calm and confident.

He turned and gestured for Anastasia to come forward. She was dressed in clean, shining armor, her ruby encrusted sword sheathed at her back and her golden hair unbound. She approached the audience with bright eyes and a soft smile across her face.

"Welcome, everyone. My name is Anastasia Brandistone," she greeted the crowd, "and believe it or not, I am one of you."

Surprised murmurs spread throughout the audience at the sight of the woman before them, glowing with the power of the Gods and very much in corporeal form. It was for this moment that Thorn had chosen her as his ally and commander, knowing the other souls would need proof that what he was about to ask of them was even possible. More than that, he needed the souls to see one of their own choosing to sacrifice their own peace to save the living. Anastasia represented hope and a bridge between mortals and immortals, souls and the living, and, as she shone brightly and confidently before the gathered souls, he couldn't have been prouder of Agnes's sister.

"I lost my fight only days ago and transitioned from my human life as a Queen to my new eternity in the Afterworld," she continued. "My family, thank the Gods, have not yet met my fate. It is for that reason, with the help of the Deities' power, that I stand before you, able to wield a sword once more as a Commander in the Gods' army. For my children and my husband, I will fight again, to give them hope of a future."

A small glimmering tear trickled down her cheek despite the confidence that she projected. Another action he had surmised would draw in the crowd with her show of vulnerability. A strategic move of a God who had fought in more wars than he could count. He did not know

164

what sort of a God that made him to use her emotions like that, but this was war.

Thorn thanked Anastasia, offering her an overly elaborate bow that he hoped would earn him favor with the crowd.

"Lilith and I have the power to raise an army of the dead, but we need your help," he declared, pausing for a moment to let the crowd settle.

"Let me be clear," he continued, his voice a resounding, husky boom. "We will only accept volunteers into our ranks. I want to emphasize that no one will be forced to fight against their will. It is not our intention to disrupt your afterlives."

The souls of departed farmers dressed in homespun garb and soldiers clad in more substantial leathers—many dented from battle— began to push their way through the crowds towards him.

"You must know, even if you join our ranks, you will not have your lives restored, nor will you be impervious to injury," Thorn said. "But if you join our army, you will fight once more for those you love most."

With an outstretched arm, he gestured for Agnes and her family to step forward. They each shone with the essence of the Gods, but only Agnes was truly blessed with the gift of immortality. As one, they all gathered atop the stairs, presenting themselves as a united front, even though Titian and Alecia, unsurprisingly, refused to make eye contact with or acknowledge Agnes's presence.

Thorn turned his attention back to the crowd. As the address went on, the crowds thinned, millions of souls returning to their eternal homes within the Afterworld to find peace.

"The Brandistone family—the former rulers of Alearia, a strong and proud Kingdom—all suffered before they lost their lives," Thorn continued, undeterred. "Yet today, they stand before you imbued with the power of the Gods, prepared to fight for loved ones who remain in Alearia to ensure that they, too, do not meet the same fates."

Mixed murmurs of approval and uncertainty rippled through the crowd.

"If you, like the family beside me, choose to fight for those who cannot defend themselves, then I ask you to step forward and raise your hand to indicate your choice to stand with us. If you wish to return to your homes in the Afterworld, your choice will be respected. We do not have the luxury of time. The Kingdoms are in desperate need of our help. Please take a moment to decide, but then we must begin the transformation process. If you choose not to assist or feel you are unable, please feel no shame in following wherever your heart leads you home," Thorn finished, dipping his head.

The Brandistone royals descended the steps to rejoin the crowd, leaving Agnes by Thorn's side. Lilith resumed her place beside him, her shadows flickering around her feet, revealing her inner turmoil like an open book despite her confident posture and hopeful smile.

Thorn took Agnes's hand, bridging the gap between them, needing to feel her. The time would come far too soon when they would be flung into battle. Even with a reborn army, the odds of success did not sit well with him. Agnes's scent of rose and woods washed over him, and he breathed it in deeply, savoring the moment, reminding him of life.

19

The Goddess of Blood and Bone

If the bones of Nushka's throne could talk, they would tell the tales of life and death. Stories of lives long-lived, stories of infants taken too soon. Tales of crime, disease, and poverty, tales of love and lust. Each bone that formed a part of her throne was taken from bodies left in the mortal realm after their souls had entered the Hall of Shadows. Each bone was a gift from her now departed father to placate her into accepting a fate that no other Deity would submit to.

The Queen of the Gods tapped her claws incessantly against the arm of her throne, taking in the dents, missing shards, and traces of dried sinew that clung from the battle wounds of their former owners. As each bone slowly degraded over time, it was replaced by another. Bones were never in short supply.

Zeri, her ghost shifter, was curled at her feet beneath the war table in giant wolf form, reminding her of the day she had brought them to The Pitts to be her pet bhoot. A faithful, loyal companion amongst a universe of snakes.

Kayla, in corporeal form, waited with chained ankles outside the chamber, ready to be called upon at a moment's notice. Nushka still preferred her former handmaiden, Agnes, but she warmed her brother's bed these days. The thought sent a wave of disgust through her. Passed on like used goods, exactly what she deserved.

To her left, Ilbis sat smugly, picking at his nails. As the oldest of Nushka's creations, he viewed himself as her second-in-command, but he didn't understand his true purpose. Whilst he was an asset to her dark army, he was still worth about as much as one of her handmaidens in the grand scheme of things. The foul stench of the ghoul commander to his left made Nushka's lip curl in disgust.

"I am sick of waiting for that bloody witch," Nushka bristled, surveying the room, tapping her claws on the marble table. "It appears she is neglecting her duties yet *again*. I could magnanimously forgive her for missing one weekly council meeting, but two weeks in a row is reprehensible."

The leaders remained silent.

The war council chamber in the Land of the Gods was stark in comparison to the opulence found elsewhere in the realm of the Deities. Unlike most open-aired rooms in the Kingdom, this windowless hall was buried in the middle of the floating castle with no natural light, causing the air to smell stale.

A row of lit torches hung in sconces along the sandstone wall, and a broad fireplace blazed on the opposite side of the chamber. It was a place for strategy and secrets—a place where universe-altering decisions were made. In a way, the claustrophobic nature of the room made Nushka feel at ease. After an eternity living in The Pitts of Moor surrounded by fire and darkness, the room deprived of natural light and clean air reminded her more of the realm in which she had called home for far too long.

"Where is she?" she hissed when no one answered, her hair flailing erratically. She looked expectantly at the Peuchen King, Xanos—a descendent of Medusa the gorgon—whose towering, onyx-scaled body, crimson wings, and long serpent tail wrapped around the room, but even he had nothing to say. His forked tongue flicked as he hissed in annoyance, but he kept his eyes closed. One look directly into his eyes would turn the source of his ire into stone, so no one challenged the serpent dragon King.

Mandigon, head of the edimmu clan—whose blue-tinged skin and emaciated form made his cheeks look sallow despite his significant strength—sat on the other side of the vacant seat to Nushka's right. Mandigon radiated an aura of power that Nushka had never witnessed in the past. The immortal who gained his strength from digesting the souls of mortals had clearly been busy in the mortal world as the war raged on.

The door to the chamber creaked open as one of the Peuchen King's guards tucked his head into the room, unable to slither his way inside for lack of room.

"Forgivvve the intrusssion your Majesssty," the peuchen guard hissed telepathically.

"What isss it, guard?" Xanos returned, mind-to-mind.

The Goddess of Blood and Bone sighed heavily through her nostrils. "Stop wasting my time and spit it out."

The guard nodded shallowly in reverence, bumping his large head with a reverberating thud on the top of the door frame and releasing a hiss in irritation.

"I wasss sss-sent to retrieve the High Witch, but shhhe isss gone," the guard answered. Even spoken telepathically, Nushka could tell the guard feared the implications of delivering unfortunate news.

She glared at Xanos's closed eyes, then turned to meet the messenger's gaze.

"Well, where is she?!"

The guard remained silent.

Below the table, Zeri huffed in response. Nushka felt him raise from her feet to slink out from the side of the table, setting between his Queen and the retrieval guard.

Ilbis snickered at her side, leaning back in his chair and enjoying the show. Nushka sent a lashing of dark magic at him to remind him who was boss. The immortal jolted in his wooden chair from the surge of sharp pain, but did not make a sound or refute his punishment. A wicked smile spread upon her lips, revealing grimy, crooked fangs.

With a sharp jerk of her chin, snake-like hair writhing in anticipation at her back, she redirected her attention to the incompetent overgrown snake dragon before her.

"I expect a logical explanation," Nushka warned. "If you are unable to provide me with one, then I am afraid the only time you will attend this war chamber again is as a dragon skin rug." Zeri growled approvingly, his hackles up as he surveyed the dragon, no doubt imagining what it would be like to morph into a creature of equal size and proportion to defend his mistress's honor. The peuchen's emerald eyes flared as Nushka said slowly. "Where. Is. Hyacinth?"

"Shhhe was last ssseen by her clan in a sssmall tttown," he answered hesitantly, his voice shaking in her mind. *"And taken by Lilithhh."*

Nushka pursed her lips, flurries of her shadows extending from the hem of her gown in search of their next victim.

"And what did my darling sister want with my High Witch?" Nushka asked, breathing in and out of her nostrils, her temper rising.

The guard squirmed within the doorway. When the grimacing dragon eventually found his telepathic voice, he murmured: *"The Wendigassst do not know, Missstresss. But therrre were thhhreatsss involved ifff the High Witchhh did not go willlllingly."*

Nushka screamed, the room exploding in a flurry of smoke and dark shadows as she unleashed her fury, allowing her powers free rein. The spare chair beside her exploded into a million shards that flew across the space. When the smoke and shadows finally dissipated, the edge of her rage dispelled, the peuchen guard, now a heap of charred flesh, lay dead, blocking the doorway. Another small thought from the Queen had the body disintegrated into ash and cleared away on a phantom wind.

"It seems my sister and I are overdue for a little chat," she seethed through gritted teeth, wild-eyed and ready to spill blood. The call to battle rose within her once more.

The Goddess of Darkness

Row upon row of souls stretched out upon the endless expanse of soft, billowing clouds. Slowly, their numbers dwindled as many dispersed to their eternal homes, unable or unwilling to partake in the outrageous plan proposed to them.

Lilith rolled her eyes as the repulsive stench of need wafted over from the two love birds. "Keep it in your pants, brother. Was one round not enough already today?"

A shockwave of his magic almost had her on her ass.

"Son of a harpy!" she hissed as Thorn scoffed, his chest puffed up with a sense of self-importance. "Arrogant alpha male."

"I can't argue with that," he chuckled before redirecting his attention back to the dwindling crowd before them.

"I can't help but wonder if we should have handled this differently," she murmured as souls left the realm in droves. Far more souls had dispersed than remained.

Thorn hummed in agreement, rubbing the stubble at his chin. "I was just thinking the same," he admitted, his usual confidence missing, "but the more I think about it, the more I realize there was never going to be a good way to ask the souls to sacrifice this peace and be thrown back into turmoil. I wouldn't be so keen to volunteer if I were in their position."

Agnes raised a brow. "Really?" she questioned unabashedly, and Thorn just shrugged.

Lilith chuckled softly but kept her musings to herself. After stretching her neck and rolling her shoulders, she stepped forward, digging deep within. Her porcelain skin glowed softly, her magic humming beneath her skin. Her strength reflected in the vigor of the shadows flailing at her feet, the prayers and worship of the souls in the Hall of Shadows still filling her well. She wondered how far it would stretch.

Now that the crowd had clustered at the foot of the stairs, the numbers stabilized, Lilith began drawing her magic to her fingertips. All hundred thousand or so remaining souls held their hands high, and Thorn stepped forward, leaving her lover behind, chin held high and lips pursed.

"First the barrier," Thorn instructed, "then we can begin."

Breathing in through his nostrils and out through his mouth, Thorn raised his arms upwards, Lilith mirroring his movements.

A surge of power erupted from them both; a final line in the sand of this war. Darkness intermingled with wind, merging to form an arch that projected from their arms and radiated into the distant horizon, dimming the bright light of the realm.

Sweat beaded at Lilith's forehead as she poured more power into the shield, pushing herself and her magic which flowed eagerly, like a geyser that had been blocked for far too long. At her side, power surged from Thorn seemingly effortlessly. It wasn't the first time she envied her brother for his ability to draw strength from the prayers of war. He was a force to be reckoned with and she was glad to have him on her side.

Together, their power played gleefully as it formed a shield across the realm. A shield not only to protect from spying eyes, but to deny Nushka access once their grand army was revealed. They both knew she would unleash her vengeance upon the Afterworld next. It was their duty to the souls to protect and serve. That was the pledge she and Thorn had made to the Afterworld upon taking over. They would not leave the souls that remained behind unguarded.

With a zing of magic reverberating down her arm—a sign that their shield could be stretched no further—Lilith released her power, a dome of murky light locking into place over the realm.

"It is done."

Thorn sighed, stretching his arms. "Now the hard work begins, sister." He turned to her, hands clenching and unclenching at his sides. "Are you ready to push your power to its limit?" he asked gently.

Lilith smiled softly at his concern. "We are in this together. When one falls, the other will be there to catch them," she promised.

Thorn nodded solemnly, then took one of her hands in his own as they faced the souls before them. Many radiated anxiety, evidenced in the small tells of a tremor or a pursed lip. But most stood with shoulders back, dressed in the colors of their former Kingdoms, their transparent armor coating their forms. A united front with their soon-to-be comrades in arms at their sides.

"You may feel an unpleasant heat flow through you or a tingling, uncomfortable sensation as we imbue you with our powers, turning spirit to flesh. Do not fear, this too shall pass," Thorn said. Many of the souls before them nodded in acceptance, a few taking a step back, a small number fading away back to their families.

"Do not fear," Lilith echoed the sentiment. "We are with you. You are not alone. We would not ask this of you unless there was another way. But worry not, as you are being reanimated by choice, you will always have the option to return to your spirit form and follow your heart's desire back to the peace of the Afterworld. We would not want you to suffer pain needlessly. We could never doom any being to a fate so horrible."

Lilith released Thorn's hand and began descending the sandstone steps shrouded in clouds, the castle she had come to call home at her back. Thorn remained a calming presence at her side, his powerless aura still radiating as strongly as it had before creating the protective shield over the realm. As they walked, Lilith expended a small amount of power, summoning a loose gown of ebony silk and discarding the skintight leathers that chafed at her skin from sweat. Comfort over practicality, this time. If she was going to push her powers further than she had before, she needed to be cool.

"Place a hand on your neighbor's shoulder. As one body and soul, one unit, you will begin to feel the winds of change. As one, you will transform into something more," Lilith explained, applying the same principles she had used on a rare occasion in the Hall of Shadows when she had lost her temper. That day, she had judged souls by groups based on her disgust for the way in which a Kingdom's people had attempted to destroy her own, rather than on an individual case-by-case basis. A weak moment she was not overly proud of.

She stopped before a young man who, for lack of a better word, seemed rather unremarkable. But his love for his family—the way he had begged on his knees, pulling at the hem of her gown—she would never forget. As he met her gaze, his name drifted to the surface of her mind. Solomon. A devout man, who, with his young wife's help, had raised their children to worship and seek guidance from their Goddess.

Solomon dropped to one knee, bowing his head in reverence. The crowd around him followed his lead in a wave of respect.

"It is good to see you, Solomon," she offered warmly.

"Thank you, my Goddess, you are too kind," he replied, his voice shaking.

"Rise. All of you," Thorn commanded, and the crowd did as he bid, resuming their contact with the souls around them.

Lilith offered Solomon a small, sad smile. "I am sorry that you have not yet been reunited with your family. You must miss them dearly."

"I do, my Goddess," he agreed, voice wavering, "But it is for them that I will fight. So that they may live when the rest of us, taken too early, have not been so fortunate."

The Goddess nodded, offering her hand for the soul to take. A former farmer-turned-soldier, dressed in proud armor marked with the red and gold colors of his home Kingdom of Alearia.

The gathered men and women from all backgrounds stood linked together in a web of solidarity. To Lilith's surprise, there were many more females present than she was expecting, though her heart broke to think of what had driven their desire to volunteer to fight in the war.

'Perhaps the absence of fear of death helped to tip the scales in our favor. Even in the most forward thinking of Kingdoms, it is unheard of to see women so well represented amongst the ranks as I see before us.'

Focusing back on the task at hand, Lilith delved deeper and deeper into the trenches of her power. She had never felt the bottom before and, truth be told, she was unsure what determined the limits on a God's powers. She could, however, recall years of being deprived of prayers and worship. Those years had felt like she was perpetually trudging through water. Deep wrinkles had set in, her hair became limp, and her shadows lacked the energy to roam or explore, reflecting the absence of vigor and strength she had felt at the time. It was a dark time in her life, one she preferred not to dwell upon. She couldn't help but think of how the Gods in the dungeons had appeared in much the same way. Without help, she feared they would soon perish.

"Lilith?" Thorn spoke softly at her side, startling her slightly. She offered him an apologetic smile. "Are you ready to begin?" he asked, resting his hand upon the shoulder of another soul Lilith recalled meeting in the Hall of Shadows. Thomas, his name was.

She gave a shallow nod.

The Goddess couldn't feel Solomon's hand in her own, so she chose to channel her power into the abyss where sensation and pain were absent, bringing life and form to the man before her. Solomon gritted his teeth as the pain began to set in, an electric shock buzzing between them where they maintained contact.

She funnelled into her power, bringing it to the surface, feeling as though her soul was shredding into a million pieces. She imbued her essence into the soul before her and every other soul thereafter, pushing herself further and further as she turned spirit to flesh, depositing a small part of herself into each new soul her power connected with. The moans of the crowd grew as the power of the Gods infused within them ushered them into the next stage of their eternal lives.

Beside her, she could feel her brother's power surging from him like a wave with no end. As his aura began to diminish ever so slightly— the only sign of the strain upon his power—the souls on his side of the crowd began pulsing with light as a trace of his power flowed through them, mirroring Lilith's.

Lilith's breathing became labored as she stretched herself further than she ever had before, her vision blurring as her head grew light and her back became slick with sweat. Beside her, Thorn's power continued to rage, replenishing as quickly as it depleted, but the well within her began to splutter, her chest tightening, barely able to maintain the intensity of the outpour of her power. She soon lost count of the number of souls she had beseeched with the gift of her essence.

Solomon, now reanimated into corporeal form, acted as a grounding point as she released his hand with a gasp before rejoining the connection by resting her hand upon his shoulder. His desperate gasps echoed her own, and the air thinned as she began pulling magic from the realm around her, desperate to bolster her own strength and powers. The shield above waivered momentarily until Thorn's power, mercifully, picked up the slack for her own, like calling to like. The smell of copper overcame her before blood began trickling from her nose. She wiped it clean with the sleeve of her gown before squeezing her eyes shut and gritting her teeth. She breathed through the pain and focused on spreading her power to the far reaches of the souls in the line of her fire. The peace of the Afterworld in this part of the realm was shattered with the moans and screams of the transforming soldiers.

The weather seemed unseasonably warm, her head swimming through clouded thoughts as she tried to keep one foot in the present.

"Thorn," Lilith panted, gasping for breath between words, "I... I can't hold on any longer." Her hand dropped from Solomon's shoulder, breaking the connection, and she opened her eyes, the realm swaying around her, her legs weak. Rocking on unsteady legs, she tried and failed to keep her footing. Solomon reached to catch her, concern etched across his face as he called her name, then the darkness embraced her.

The God of War

The prayers and worship of those still clinging to life echoed through Thorn's body, restoring his strength like an endless power source to draw from. As life and death met in the most intimate of ways, souls were reunited with their former corporeal forms and the army building before him gave him a sense of hope. He had felt Lilith's strength wane, the power flowing from her a mere echo of the inundation that had blasted from her in the beginning. It was no surprise when she landed in a heap at his feet, even the sound of the growing army unable to wake her.

Dark, billowing clouds began to fill the sky surrounding the protective shield that he maintained with an echo of his power. Without Lilith to assist with the transformation, Thorn released the damper on his power, pouring out his magic—his soul—at a nearly unimaginable rate. Even with the steady stream of prayers and worship reaching him, he knew he couldn't maintain this level of intensity for much longer, but thankfully, he didn't have to.

Lifting his head across the now glowing crowd of corporeal soldiers, he pushed his essence into the final rows of souls awaiting their transformation. He knitted bone and flesh together similarly to tending battle wounds in the field. Only, in this instance, his magic was creating whole bodies. The souls were imbued with the blood and strength of the God of War himself.

Thorn fell to his knees, taking a moment to catch his breath as the final few souls reanimated. Only then did he let his gaze settle upon his sister.

"Lil," he said, shaking her shoulder to rouse her. He pressed two fingers to her wrist, her pulse thankfully thrumming with the intensity of a thousand stampeding horses. "Lilith," he called, trying fruitlessly to rouse her.

Dejectedly, he rose to one knee and lifted his siter into his arms, an overprotective move she would curse him for if she was awake. As he left the crowd of now eagerly chatting would-be soldiers, he opened a small portal, carrying his sister from the safety and confines of the Afterworld into a realm of chaos.

The Hall of Shadows, filled with souls awaiting their eternal judgement, went silent as The God of War entered, carrying the Goddess of Darkness gently in his arms. He lay her upon the throne of bones, summoning a soft pillow to rest her head on and a fur blanket to warm her cooled limbs. Thorn tucked her in tight and turned to the awestruck souls that awaited his next move.

"Welcome to the Hall of Shadows. The Goddess of Darkness—the woman before you—is your only hope of an eternity shrouded in peace. Worship her with all your being and do not stop until she glows like a beacon, and even then, over the coming days and weeks, do not stop. She needs your prayers just as much as you need her favor.

Help her and, in turn, she will help you and your families still fighting in the mortal Kingdoms."

As if a fire had been set upon the realm, the souls before him dropped to their knees and broke out into prayer and worship. A cacophony of sound filled the Hall that would act as a power source for his sister to regain her strength. Thankfully, it would not be long until Lilith would rejoin him. A hint of color was already returning to her fine features, though her shadows remained dormant.

After depositing Lilith in the Hall of Shadows—the only place she could regain her strength in such a short period of time—Thorn returned to the Afterworld through a tiny crack in the barrier he created to travel through quickly, sealing the gap behind him as soon as he was safely inside.

Re-appearing upon the makeshift dais at the entrance to the open-aired castle, Thorn was momentarily struck speechless, a rare moment indeed. Agnes approached his side, biting her lip, suppressing a laugh at the unfolding events. Her family quietly talked amongst themselves nearby, avoiding making awkward eye contact with anyone in the crowd.

A low chuckle escaped him that quickly grew into a gruff, full belly laugh as he turned to face Agnes. She chuckled as she gnawed on her lip, trying and spectacularly failing to regain her composure. It appeared that many of the departed needed a moment or two to revel in the freedom of having returned to their corporeal forms, fully embracing the sensation of touch in its most decadent form. A celebration to rival those of Nushka's evenings of debauchery broke out amongst a large proportion of the crowds. Thorn had the feeling many were former lovers, now reunited in every sense of the word. Others seemed content exploring and enjoying the moment, lost to lust and their baser urges.

"I think they may need a moment before our greatest hopes for the Kingdoms are ready to answer my call to arms," Thorn chuckled, waggling his eyebrows at his lover.

Agnes's answering laugh was music to his ears. She shook her head in astonishment. "Gosh, I don't remember being that lost to lust after I gained my immortal life."

"Well, my dear, I think you and I have different memories of these past months, because you and I are exactly like that," he quipped.

Agnes blushed, turning her head away, "I don't know what you're talking about. I am the epitome of self-control."

"Ha! Keep telling yourself that, sweetheart." He rolled his eyes.

Agnes scoffed, "Well, now that you mention it... Lilith is currently indisposed, and your grand army of the risen dead are busy attending to their *needs*. Shall we retire for a few hours and come back once the dust has settled?"

His pants felt a size too small. "I don't see why not. We need to rest. We have a big battle ahead of us after all." He shrugged his shoulders. "It would be irresponsible not to, really."

Agnes's answering grin had him shaking his head slightly in disbelief. "You're a bad influence on me, Princess," he teased.

She feigned shock, bringing a hand to her chest, mouth agape. "I don't know what you're talking about. I only have your best interests at heart."

"Of that my darling, I have no doubt..."

With a wave of his hand, he erected several dozen tables amongst the army. Another thought had them laden with delicacies from all Kingdoms, piled a foot high. The rich aroma of roasted meats and vegetables wafted through the air. He withheld the wine and ale though, needing his army alert. The answering cheers from the remaining, undistracted soldiers resounded through the crowd.

A separate table, lined with chairs and donned with silver cutlery and fresh crisp linens, appeared beside the Brandistone family, laden with the familiar foods of their home Kingdom of Alearia. A small decanter of the wine of the gods appeared upon their table. Not enough to intoxicate, but enough to help them relax and take the edge off their anxiety. A smile and nod from Amealiana were all the acknowledgement he needed as he took his lover's hand in his own and escorted her inside.

22

Agnes

Her heart raced in her chest as hand-in-clammy-hand they meandered through the blessedly peaceful castle, with only the sounds of their light-footed steps keeping them company. Agnes took a deep breath, exhaling slowly through her nose. The sweet, calming scent of lavender floated through the air as the realm anticipated her needs. It never ceased to amaze her how a realm created to harbor the dead could be so rich with life. The perfect place for her heart to heal from the trauma of her life and afterlife in The Pitts of Moor.

Rather than stopping at the entry leading to their suite, Thorn led her farther into the heart of the castle, ascending staircase after cloud-shrouded staircase. Finally, they reached the top level where a circular sunroom sat perched amongst the clouds. An archway led out onto a balcony, the walls lined with floor-to-ceiling wooden bookshelves, a rainbow of books of every genre vying for space. Two oversized red velvet chairs and a side table sat adjacent, a decanter of wine and crystal glassware sitting on top. The rich bouquet of the wine filled the room, and Agnes released a contented sigh.

"Shall I pour us some wine?" Thorn asked, already leading her over to the two chairs.

"Yes, please," she replied softly, taking a seat on one of the over-stuffed lounges.

As Thorn poured them each a generous glass, Agnes took a moment to savor the peace of the space, treasuring the quiet moment away from the judgmental eyes of her family and the overwhelming intensity of the army her lover had raised.

The first sip from the glass Thorn passed her tasted so glorious she moaned softly before taking another, delighting in the taste. Thorn smiled sleepily at her in return as half his glass disappeared all too quickly.

He clicked his fingers and, to her surprise, a musician appeared with a harp where, just moments before, one of the chairs had been. The sprite began playing a song that told the story of a lover's journey—a song she recalled hearing at balls during her childhood. The music filled her with hope. Thorn gulped down the remainder of his glass and set it aside on the table, offering her his hand.

"May I have this dance?" he asked, bowing for her.

A few small sips later and Agnes was feeling as light as a cloud, heat pooling in her stomach as the music and the wine of the gods unburdened her of her worries. Setting aside her glass, she took Thorn's calloused hand and allowed him to escort her outside, a cloud of his darkness curtaining off the sunroom. As he pulled her into his embrace, she rested her head against his chest as they danced beneath the clouds, abandoning all thoughts of the army and battle awaiting them.

Agnes lifted her head, looking up in awe at the God who held her heart. His returning smile made her heart ache, and he leant down to press his soft lips to her own. She opened to him, and Thorns kissed her with such tenderness that it threatened to be her undoing.

The music called to them and they drew closer as they danced, tasting and cherishing the time they had together. Thorn's hand was a soothing presence at her back, his other buried in her hair as their kiss transformed into something of desperation and longing, as if this were to be their last untainted, peaceful moment together.

She pulled away. "This cannot be the end, Thorn, promise me," she commanded, a tear trickling down her cheek. "No matter what happens, what danger lies ahead, promise me that we will always be together."

Silver lined his eyes. "I will love you always, but not even the fates know what is in store. But know that even if the worst comes to pass and the ether or The Pitts claim me, I will always find my way back to you. Always."

Tears flowed freely now. "I cannot lose you, Thorn. I just can't."

Thorn smiled softly. "My love, our hearts will always be joined. Even if the sun sets on our final day amongst the living, the sun will always rise upon our eternity amongst the souls. One way or another, we will be together, forever."

Agnes kissed him again, needing to taste him, to know they were still alive, that this wasn't all a dream and they still had time.

Thorn's hand roved down her back and grasped her ass. She moaned as his pants strained against the front of her gown and his other hand slipped between them to grasp her chest. Heat built in her core, and with her lover's help she discarded her gown and his hands continued exploring her body. A moment later, his clothes misted away in a cloud of smoke, allowing her better access to him.

He lifted her as she wrapped her legs around his waist and gently set her upon the top of the sandstone balcony ledge. The moment reminded her of the first time he had worshipped her during the ball, before the universe had ascended into chaos. The tenderness and care he had shown for her then had ripped down her emotional walls and renewed her faith in love again.

As Thorn tore his mouth from hers, he began trailing kisses along her jaw, pausing to nibble on her ear lobe, before continuing his exploration ever so slowly down her neck, taunting her with his tongue. She stretched her neck to allow him better access, but he continued his journey, kissing along her shoulder, then painstakingly slowly down her chest. She stilled as his kisses trailed lower, one hand massaging her breast, the other grasped around her inner thigh, just out of reach of where she wanted him most.

A guttural groan escaped him as she wrapped one hand around his length and drew him closer so that his slick tip just barely touched her entrance. Legs still wrapped around his waist, the pulsing of him against her had her desperate for more, his length growing tauter in her hand with each movement.

His mouth wrapped around her nipple, sucking and taunting her with his tongue. She arched into him, increasing the pressure and speed at which she tended to him. Unable to deny her any longer, Thorn moved his other hand from her thigh, forcing her to detangle herself from him. He parted her legs so that he could slip his fingers into her slick entrance, massaging the delicate bundle of nerves with his thumb. She gasped, pulling her mouth away from his, releasing his cock to grab hold of his shoulders to steady herself as he lowered himself from her breast and knelt before her to taste her.

The first lick of his tongue had her pleading for more. Each frustratingly slow, playful movement felt like torture, drawing out her pleasure, but also making her beg for more. When she could take it no longer, she pulled at his shoulders, urging him upwards and pulling him closer until he pushed against her entrance.

"Please," she breathed.

"Please, what?" he whispered in her ear, inching himself ever so slightly inside her.

"Please," she whimpered. "Just fuck me!" She groaned, grabbing his ass and pulling him closer.

Thorn chuckled darkly before he sucked at her neck just below her ear, the action sending a fresh wave of heat flooding through her.

"As you wish, my darling," he whispered, wrapping one hand around her back. He gave her one last massage with the other before thrusting himself all the way in, not giving her time to adjust. She gasped. He withdrew almost fully before slamming back in. On and on, hard and fast, he made every movement count. Only the two of them existed in that moment. A cloud of Thorn's darkness blocked out the universe, depriving them of most of their vision and heightening all other senses.

Agnes's breathing became ragged as she slipped her hand between them and began massaging her clit as he continued to fuck her with such urgency and desperation it made her heart clench. He released a moan of approval as he watched her tend to her own needs, writhing beneath her own touch. He palmed her breast with his free hand, her nipple taut beneath his touch.

Their lips met again, their kisses forceful and demanding. As she felt her climax draw near, her heart raced and she gasped, pulling away and flinging her head back, her sandy hair a wave behind her, flowing out over the balcony's edge. Thorn sucked and teased at her neck as she kept massaging herself, the pressure building within. Uncontainable pants and moans escaped her as her climax flooded through her, her moans turning to a guttural scream.

"Yes, my love," Thorn panted, "embrace it." He increased his pace, using his free hand to circle her clit as she rode out each rippling wave of ecstasy, gasping for breath.

A moment later he dropped his hand and grasped her shoulder to steady himself, his gasps now mirroring her own and, with one hard thrust, he roared to sky as he came. As he slowed his pace, drawing out each final pleasurable moment for them both, Agnes pressed soft, sweet kisses to his neck, drawing him into her embrace.

Finally, he stilled and dropped his head to rest upon her shoulder, holding her just as tightly as she held him, his heart racing and breathing ragged, echoing her own.

"I'm not ready for this to end," she whispered, leaning her head against his.

"Neither am I," Thorn whispered, squeezing her a little tighter.

She inhaled his scent, committing his smoky, woodsy aroma to memory. The sound of the harp had ceased, the musician having likely taken their leave long ago to give them privacy. The sound of the crowd far, far, below filtered up through the clouds.

Pulling out of her embrace, Thorn straightened and took her by the waist to slowly and gently lower her from the balcony ledge, her legs a little wobbly and her head light.

He lover summoned a portal and, taking her by the hand, he led her through the wave of light into *their* suite. No longer did he call it his own and no longer did she feel as if she was intruding upon his private space to share it with him. The smell of lavender again wafted over her as they entered the bathing chamber where a steaming tub filled with bubbly hot water awaited them.

"I know the soothing water brings you calm. I thought you might like to relax for a while," he offered softly.

Agnes, suddenly acutely aware of her nakedness, found herself wishing she had a wrap of some kind. She looked up at him, smiling softly before gently biting her lip. "Only if you would join me?" she asked, feeling the heat rise to her cheeks despite all they had shared.

"You needn't ask. There is nowhere else I would rather be," he chuckled as he swept her into his arms and stepped into the oversized tub built for two. He gently set her down before him so that she could sit comfortably with her back to his chest.

Upon the small side table beside the bath, an array of wash cloths, oils, soaps, and hair products appeared, the floral scents intermingling with the scent of lavender already flooding the chamber. Thorn chose a small vial that smelled like roses and lathered his hands, massaging her with it. The warm oil and the hot water kept all other thoughts at bay.

"You'll have to be careful, or a girl could get used to being treated like this," she chuckled, arching into his touch, releasing a soft moan of contentment.

"Oh, my darling, this is nothing," he huskily replied, massaging her shoulders. "I thoroughly intend to ravage you like a Queen for the rest of our never-ending existence." He playfully bit her ear lobe before reacquainting himself with her neck, sending a ripple of heat through her core.

"Hmmm, I think I like the sound of that," she hummed sleepily. "But only as long as I get to return the favor."

"I would love nothing more."

Agnes turned, cupping his cheek with her hand. She braced her other on Thorn's shoulder, learning forward to press her lips to his, parting his mouth with her tongue and deepening the kiss. Her hand began to rove down his chest ever so slowly, returning the taunting he had gifted her with earlier. One of his hands wrapped around her waist, the other tangling in her hair.

"Can I do something for you?" she asked, hand continuing its journey, her mouth suddenly dry.

"Anything," he replied, eyes bright.

Without warning, a resounding boom echoed through the realm and Agnes hastily clamped her hands over her ears to stop the ringing. A moment later the castle amongst the clouds began to shake. In a cloud of darkness, Thorn was out of the tub and dressed in his armor. His wavy hair still damp from the water.

"I need you to get dressed, but stay here. I'm going to find out what in the realm is going on and then I will come back for you. I promise."

Dread pooled in her stomach and her heart raced. There wasn't enough air in the room.

"Take me with you. I want to help."

"I love you," he whispered, leaning down to press a brief kiss to her lips. "Stay safe," In a blur of his shadows, he left Agnes, naked and alone.

The God of War

The Afterworld had ascended into chaos. Billowing storm clouds filled the late afternoon sky. Lightning and whips of darkness slammed into the protective shield with all the rage of the Queen of the Gods, causing the realm to tremor with each lashing. Breathing deeply, Thorn took in the sight of the fissures spreading like a spider's web across the outer layers of the dome.

Calling upon his darkness, the scent of smoke and ash filling the air, the God of War summoned the cache of weapons he had been hiding away over the past weeks. All of it in preparation for this moment. A day that had come far too soon and without Lilith by his side. He had not anticipated an attack so soon. Centuries of walking on and off battlefields, however, had taught him to be flexible and adapt to all conditions, so that was exactly what he would do.

Hands fisted, Thorn called upon his power, funneling deeply, drawing forth his deadly shadows and fierce winds until they danced at his fingertips, eager to be unleashed. To buy his army time enough to depart the realm and draw Nushka's dark army away, he had no choice but to expend the extra energy needed to reinforce the realm's shield. To protect and serve was the code he lived by, and he would not let the souls of the Afterworld down.

He lifted his hands towards the raging storm and unleashed himself, teeth bared, arms and legs trembling as wave after wave of his dark power thrust into the shield, knitting cracks and fissures together. Thorn flung the raging tempest that was his darkness at the protective barrier, his breath becoming increasingly labored, but with each new fissure his magic healed, a new crack started to show. It was like a dog chasing his own tail and he knew his efforts would be futile in the end. What was one God against the might of a Dark Queen such as Nushka and an army of mythical beasts?

His brow furrowed under the strain of expelling so much power at such an intense rate. "Anastasia!" he ground out through clenched teeth.

The former mortal Queen was at his side moments later, concern etched across her face. Sword in hand, her hair was braided back and more weapons were strapped to her. She looked every inch the ruler of the people.

"What's our strategy?" she demanded, her clear, blue-eyed gaze constantly shifting between him and the failing shield above them.

"Now is your time to shine, Commander. Gather your family and lead the troops out of here. Many of those souls are former soldiers and will obey without question. You will be a formidable force, I assure you."

Anastasia's eyes widened, but she listened intently, nodding at his orders.

"I will maintain the barrier and open a portal to transport the army to Alearia. I'm not sure how much longer I can hold, so I need you to tell the troops to arm themselves before they pass through the portal. I will hold the gateway open for as long as I can, but you need to go *now*," he gasped as he struggled to bear the strain.

"I thought you were coming with us! We can't do this without you, we need you," she said, sounding exasperated.

"I need to retrieve Lilith and the High Witch who can restore my kin's powers. After that, I will join you," Thorn swore between short, sharp breaths. "I appointed you as a Commander for a reason. You can do this. I believe in you, Anastasia."

Both flinched as a rumble reverberated through the Afterworld, causing the clouds beneath their feet to shift as Nushka and her followers continued their assault upon the dome. Thorn groaned, breathing raggedly as he pushed more of his power into the shield. A battle of willpower. If it were not for the prayer and worship of the suffering mortals still clinging to hope in the Kingdoms, he would have succumbed to the darkness by now, just as Lilith had. For the first time in a very long time, he felt vulnerable.

Anastasia gave him a curt nod. "Consider it done," she replied before running off to carry out his orders.

Thorn took a deep breath as the pain of pushing himself beyond his usual limits sapped his energy to an all-time low. Gritting his teeth, he tried to breathe through it, unsure how he would muster the strength to maintain a portal whilst simultaneously protecting the Afterworld with his shield.

Tough choices would need to be made.

"Rally the troops!" he heard Anastasia call from afar. Alecia echoed her call to arms and the army fell into ranks as if on instinct, or by following the lead of those around them.

Blocking out all distractions, Thorn lowered his left arm, inch by inch, until it was parallel with the ground. With his focus, he struggled to maintain the intensity at which he repaired and reinforced the dome.

"Son of a centaur—keep it together!" he screamed to the ether.

Drawing forth more strength from an uncharted abyss within him, Thorn flung open a doorway to the mortal realm with a flare of blinding light. As the light settled, the devastation awaiting them on the other side was revealed—a destruction and chaos worse than any he could recall witnessing. The Kingdom, desolated beyond belief, almost resembling The Pitts. A level of unfathomable disaster that his army was largely unprepared for, but it was the only hope the mortals had. It would have to do. The time for planning and strategizing had run out. Ready or not, they had to go now.

24

Anastasia

The army stretched for miles as they marched, two by two, through the God's portal to Alearia. Each soul glowed with the power of the Gods, restored to their former glory, if only for a short while.

"Stay together," Alecia called from the other side of the gateway, dividing the souls into smaller legions as they passed through. The leader they needed to take control. "Our strength lies in our numbers. Together we are stronger, so stay with your legion. Guard each other's backs and do not fear what has already been taken from you." Their father, Titian Brandistone, and brother, Alexander, led the first ranks up the mountain, beneath the cover of the trees that led to Brandistone castle, their former home. If any survivors remained, they would be stranded and barricaded inside. Anastasia prayed they were not too late.

Fire flashed on the ground and in the sky, and screeches and roars could be heard through the portal's expanse.

"Stay alert," Anastasia warned the army as they made their way through the gateway. "Take two weapons each and no more. You can scavenge whatever else you find in the Kingdoms. March on with confidence, knowing that, together, we are going to make the world a better place for those we left behind."

Her stomach churned as she repeated the call to arms that she'd made countless times before, attempting to rally the ranks of soldiers made up of ordinary citizens and fighters alike as they traversed through the gateway.

Amealiana, standing tall and proud by her side, was a steadying force. She had never seen her mother fight, though Tash hoped that the training she'd had growing up would have been imparted to her mother, too. Anastasia had never had a chance to say goodbye to her mother before she passed in Alearia, and she thanked the Gods for reuniting them for all eternity. If death beckoned at their doorstep, she would never have allowed her mother to step onto the killing fields, but for her family still living amongst the chaos, and with the fear of their demise, she stood confidently at her mother's side, ready to defend their Kingdom together.

"Stand tall," Amealiana called in her soothing tone. "March proudly. You are the hope of our people and, together, we will bring peace to the many Kingdoms."

Annie, her beloved twin, stood calmy and confidently on Tash's other side. She was not a fighter, having only been trained in the most basic of self-defense techniques, but if it wasn't for her, the peace and prosperity Alearia had experienced in recent years would not have been possible. It was thanks to Annie and her mind conqueror gifting that Alearia was triumphant during the last attempted invasion of their Kingdom. Annie had sacrificed herself for her people during that battle, and though she wouldn't fight in the battle ahead, she would lead any survivors to safety. She would be a calming presence amongst the chaos, just as she had been for Anastasia during the Crowning trials and, more recently, upon her ascension into the Afterworld.

Storms raged against the barrier above, bolts of lightning, slashes of darkness, and vibrant blue flames surging with vengeance. Thorn stood nearby, sweat beading across his forehead, a grimace on his face as he strained to keep the portal open whilst maintaining his protective shield. Anastasia prayed to him silently, beseeching his strength to hold out.

The portal started to flicker, closing and re-opening at will as Thorn fell to his knees from the weight of his tasks. Anastasia and Annie rushed to his side.

"Thorn!" Annie exclaimed, kneeling beside him and helping him settle more comfortably on the ground. "You need to rest. Just take a moment," she said.

Thorn looked shattered as he raised his chin to meet her gaze, his chest heaving.

Anastasia grabbed his free shoulder and shook him. "You need to focus. I know you're tired, but we are almost there. Just hold on a little longer and then you can rest. There's only a hundred or so souls left. You just need to hang on long enough for them to make the journey through the portal!"

He looked at her sadly, shaking his head. "If I waste all my energy now, I'll be no good to anyone on the battlefield. We need to be practical. The remaining souls will need to stay here. I can't waste any more strength on the dead, I need to save it for the living!"

Anastasia's heart raced. "You can't be serious," she cried in dismay. "I need to get to my family! You promised me that I could help them! You are a *fucking* God, your power is endless! So, keep that damned portal open so we can pass through and then you can have your pity party!"

Thorn scoffed. A flash of his power had her releasing his shoulder and flying several feet through the air. She was dumped unceremoniously on her rear end. "Ouch! You son-of-a-centaur!" she screamed, scrambling to her feet and rushing back to his side. When he held his hand up to silence her, she stopped abruptly.

"I will open the portal long enough for you to travel, but everyone else will need to stay behind to protect the Afterworld," he explained with a heavy sigh.

Anastasia's eyes widened as she followed Thorn's gaze to the barrier above. Deep cracks were cracking all over the surface.

Annie met her gaze. "You need to go, Tash, go and save your family," she urged.

Understanding dawned upon her. "You're coming with me! I am not leaving you behind!"

"Safe travels, Anastasia, I will see you soon," was all Thorn offered before opening a new portal, just big enough for one person.

"No!" she cried, dropping to her knees. "I can't leave you all behind to suffer Nushka's wrath!"

"It is not your choice," Thorn responded breathlessly and, with a gust of wind, he pushed her through the portal of blinding light and slammed it shut behind her.

*

Landing with a thud on the slushy snow, Anastasia cursed the God of War as she lifted herself from the cold, wet ground and took in the familiar surroundings of the Alearian forest bordering the castle. The legion was several hundred feet ahead of her, weaving their way through the giant oak trees, weapons at the ready.

After giving her heart a moment to settle, she pursued her fellow soldiers. The rear of the guard was no place for a Commander to lead. Closing the gap between herself and the legion, she unsheathed a dagger, deeming it safer and lighter to carry through the terrain than her broad sword which was strapped across her back... not that a dagger would do much against a snake dragon, but the weapon was a comfort all the same. A chimera's roar coming from about a mile away had her increasing her pace. She needed to find Alecia and, together, they needed to find her family.

"Hold on, Cimmeris, I am coming for you," she whispered into the air, clinging to the hope that she would find them alive.

As she trudged through the slushy snow in heavy greaves, she found herself quickly regretting having all her senses restored in such a potent way. For the first time—both in her human life and now--she felt truly cold. As a fire wielder in her former life, feeling the harsh bite of winter was a strange and unfamiliar sensation.

Whilst frost bite and critical wounds could not end her existence, as she was already a resident of the Afterlife, the pain would still linger. It was the pain she wanted to avoid at all costs. She tried to reassure herself that, regardless of her promise to lead Thorn's army, she could always make the choice to return to her spirit form if she couldn't go on any longer. But if they did not win this war, the Afterworld would be the last place she would want to return.

'Regardless of the cost, we must win this war. The Goddess of Blood and Bone must be stopped.'

25

The God of War

The first drop of rain upon his head told Thorn they were well and truly fucked. The easiest thing to do would have been to rally his strength and portal out of there, but without Hyacinth, they would have no hope of restoring the Gods' powers. If today had taught him anything, it was that he was still just one God.

With one arm slung around Annie and Amealiana's shoulders for support, they began hobbling back towards the castle entrance. The last portal he had created for Anastasia took more out of him than he cared to admit. He cursed himself a fool for thinking he could do this alone.

Agnes, dressed in fighting leathers, came bursting out of the castle, almost crashing straight into him.

"What in the God's name happened to you?" she screamed, taking in his disheveled appearance.

Thorn huffed a laugh. "I've just been busy saving the world. Sorry, I hadn't had a chance to come and find you yet."

Agnes slapped him in the face, her mother gasping in horror at the misstep, but Thorn just laughed. "I missed you too," he sighed.

She rolled her eyes. "I have been busy retrieving your partner for you, since I figured you would need some backup," she said with a raised brow assessing him from head to toe.

Hyacinth stood behind her, alongside one of the last people he had thought he would find in the Afterworld. Thorn blinked several times.

"Surprise!" Admetos smirked, glowing like a veritable candle.

"I assume Hyacinth healed you?" Thorn said, tilting his head to the side.

The God of Fire lifted a hand, a single vibrant flame appearing. "I was the wretch unlucky enough to be her test subject," he replied, glaring pointedly at the witch. Then he turned his attention back to Thorn. "You look like something the chimera dragged in." He scoffed, looking down his nose at him.

Thorn wanted nothing more than to punch Admetos square in the face, but he resisted his urges.

'Allies. We need allies, Thorn,' Lilith would have reprimanded him.

Thorn clenched his teeth so hard his jaw began to hurt. "I'll admit, you're not exactly the first person I would have considered for Hyacinth's little experiments." He turned to Hyacinth, who looked as if she was ready to flatten them both. In his current state, she very well could do. "Thank you, Hyacinth. We are forever in your debt."

Hyacinth nodded. "Create a better world for the Wendigast and we shall call ourselves even," she said, handing him a vial and a scroll with a hand-scrawled incantation and instructions.

"You didn't have to help us, but you did. So, thank you. We are eternally grateful."

Hyacinth smiled, a redback spider crawling down the side of her face. "Fail us, God," she added, looking down her nose, taking in his obviously weakened state with no small amount of satisfaction, "and I will haunt you no matter which realm you call home. I will rip your little lover to shreds and feast upon her heart, savoring the taste whilst you, gagged and bound with my vines, are forced to watch."

Thorn chuckled as he beckoned Amealiana and Annie to release him. "I will not let you down."

"Shall I portal you back to your realm, High Witch?" Admetos asked, offering her an arm. "Since my cousin is in no state to summon a gentle breeze, let alone transport someone as valuable such as yourself. Time is of the essence."

Thorn rolled his eyes, nausea roiling at the God's pathetic attempt at flattery. *'Admetos really will fuck anything with two legs.'*

"I will allow it," she surmised, her tone dripping with condescension.

Admetos snickered, offering the High Witch an exaggeratedly low bow and flourish of his hand, opening a portal by his side which led to a small river village in one of the mortal Kingdoms. Thorn had no idea how he'd managed to locate her kin so quickly.

"I am glad to be of service, High Witch," the God of Fire offered.

Hyacinth strode through the gateway without hesitation and disappeared, the portal closing behind her with a flash of light.

"You had better pray to the universe that this spell works, Admetos, or I'll hold you fully responsible for dragging her back here by her spindly hair. I pray to the universe that she curses you with a hemorrhoid while you are at it," Thorn said.

Admetos crossed his arms across his chest. "Of course, it's the right spell. It worked on me." The God scoffed, picking an invisible speck of dust from the impeccably polished armor he wore. From the way he held himself, Thorn guessed whatever wounds Admetos had sustained in the dungeons had since been healed either by his own blood or the spells of the witch. '*Interesting...*' he mused.

"Just because she restored your strength does not mean she did us the consideration of providing us with the correct spell to heal the others," he explained, as if to a child.

The realm flashed with light, a crack of lightning striking the ground. They all stared above. Nushka's army was finally ready to make their grand entrance into the Afterworld.

"Well, fuck."

"Agreed, cousin," Thorn said. As his strength returned, he straightened, turning to Annie and Amealiana. "Would you like to come with us or stay here?"

Annie looked at her mother, a silent conversation passing between them. Amealiana nodded, then turned to Thorn. "We'll stay. We are needed here."

A moment later, both ladies returned to their spirit forms as Thorn drew back the spark of life he had imbued in them both. They looked at him, their mouths parted in shock.

"Why did you change us back? Did we do something wrong?" Annie gasped, placing a hand over her still heart.

Before Thorn could explain, Agnes stepped to his side and offered him a small, thankful smile. "You have done nothing wrong. You have suffered enough in your past lives, and we do not want to see you go through that again. Both of you deserve better than that. You can still help by being a reassuring presence and providing a supportive ear, but you can do both of those things in your spirit forms where you will feel no pain," she explained gently, silver lining her eyes.

"But we can't fight like this. We can't help," Annie said, taking another step.

"You have done enough already," Thorn offered gently.

"I hate to interrupt this touching situation," Admetos remarked, his tone wavering, "but we need to get out of here. That barrier is going to come down at any moment and the first thing they target will be us."

Thorn nodded. "We need to retrieve Lilith from the Hall of Shadows, then we can go to The Pitts and free the Gods," Thorn said.

Admetos raised a brow. "As you wish." With a flourish of his hand, a portal opened by their sides, the edges of it glowing like smoldering coals. With an overexaggerated flourish, he added, "After you…"

26

The Goddess of Darkness

There were two things in life of which Lilith was certain. The first was that her head had never hurt so much in her entire existence. The second was that she was going to kill Thorn for locking her out of the Afterworld with his reinforced barrier.

She tried to stretch upon her throne of bone as she woke, only to find herself tucked in like a child. It was the last situation she imagined herself being in when she had woken up that morning. The day's events felt like a blur. The last thing she remembered was assisting Thorn to reanimate the army before the darkness had embraced her fully and she had succumbed.

The chorus of prayers and worship from the souls knelt at the foot of her dais were a relentless buzzing in her ear that did little to relieve the pulsing in her head. Even the dim light of the candles suspended in the air was too much for her to handle, adding to the pain.

Still feeling weak, Lilith moved to sit upright in her throne but did not yet attempt to rise. Mouth dry, she summoned a carafe of water and drank deeply, not even bothering with a glass, before allowing her eyes to rest. Trying to block out the noise of the souls' petitions, she instead focused on her breathing, absorbing the power that came from their praise, renewing her strength. As each minute passed, her crushing headache began to slowly subside, and a spark of life returned to her shadows. Another few hours of rest and she was sure she would feel much better, but time was not on her side.

With all the power she could summon, she attempted to open a small portal, desperate to return to the Afterworld. But try as she might, the connection kept slamming closed like a vice. It was then that her palms began to sweat, her already racing heart pushing even harder.

"You will permit me to pass," she demanded of the barrier encasing the Afterworld, re-attempting breathlessly to push past the block imposed upon her. "You were created by both of us, you *will* allow me to pass through."

After fruitlessly pushing with all her might, trying to keep the gateway open long enough to pass through, she slouched back in her chair, defeated.

"Son of a centaur!" she cursed.

Shaking her head, she released a heavy sigh. The only reason she wouldn't be permitted to pass into the Afterworld would be if her power had been dwarfed by another. Thorn.

'But did he lock me out just to protect me? Or was it from necessity?'

Thrumming her fingers on the arm of the throne, she tried to remain level-headed and calm.

'What I wouldn't give to use my gift right now! Not knowing what's happening is almost as cruel as learning bad news. But a gift of discernment is useless if the subject isn't near.'

A flash of blinding light had her standing at attention, an arm shielding her eyes from the glare that sent a painful shock straight to her already raging headache. She ground her teeth, fists clenched, blood pooling in her hand as her sharp nails cut through her skin.

"You prick!" she screamed, torn between fury and relief as she launched herself at the God of War when he entered on unsteady legs through the portal.

Wrapping her arms around the God's waist, she pulled him into the tightest hug she had ever shared. A grunt sounded in her ear as he rested his head against her shoulder.

"You look a sight better than when I deposited your bony ass here a while ago," he chuckled, wrapping his arms around her in return.

Lilith groaned, loosening her grip on him slightly. "And you looked significantly cockier and more carefree the last time I saw you," she quipped, poking him in the side.

Thorn gave her one last squeeze before pulling back with a sigh, a contemplative look upon his face.

Light flared behind him, the portal slamming shut with Admetos and Agnes now at his side.

Admetos surveyed the Hall of Shadows, smirking as he took in the countless souls squeezed into the hall, their transparent feet mingling amongst the smoky, clouded floor, the candles floating in the otherwise dark space providing the only source of lighting. Turning from them to appraise her throne, he whistled low.

"I see you're just as dramatic in your styling choices as your sister," he said, smirking obnoxiously.

"I'm regretting freeing you already, Admetos," she said tiredly. "Although..." she raised her voice enough to be heard over the monotonous worship, appraising him in turn from head to toe, taking in the bright aura radiating from him. "At least you were useful for something. I see Hyacinth finally decided to be helpful."

Admetos looked down his nose. "*Please...* if it wasn't for me your brother would be peuchen food by now. Count yourself fortunate that I was there to open a functional portal."

Lilith's nostrils flared as she looked pointedly at Thorn, tilting her head. "Explain."

Agnes stepped up to his side, placing a reassuring hand in his. "I'm not sure now is the time."

Thorn nodded. "Agreed... That trip down memory lane will have to wait for another time. For now, we need to get to The Pitts, rescue the others and restore their powers. I have sent the army in blind, and the sooner we can join them the better."

Lilith nodded, taking a deep breath as her mind raced. The sounds of souls worshiping droned through the Hall and she breathed in their praise, feeling her strength slowly return with each moment. Thorn too, appeared less pale, his aura growing with every passing moment.

"Shall I open us a portal?" Admetos asked smugly.

Lilith glared at him, but swallowed her retort.

"Be our guest," Thorn said. "It's about time you started contributing a little more to our '*save the universe from certain destruction*,' campaign." Agnes barked a laugh and Lilith chuckled, but counted herself fortunate that, in her current state, she was not the one drawing the ire of the God of Fire.

Admetos sent a blaze of fire at Agnes—all light and no heat—a party trick. But it was enough to make Agnes squeal like a frightened little girl until it dawned upon her moments later that it was all smoke and mirrors. Suddenly, Lilith found herself feeling a heck of a lot better.

27

Agnes

A sliver of sweat trailed down Agnes's back, a tremor running through her fingertips that she masked by crossing her arms. A dagger was strapped to her leg, a sword to her back, the same way she and her siblings had always worn weapons when training. Her heart rate quickened as she followed Thorn, Admetos and Lilith through the portal from the relative safety of the Hall of Shadows into the heart of enemy territory... and the place she wished she could erase from her memory.

She was still haunted by the phantom pain of burns and blisters that she'd received when she was trapped in the dungeons. Now that she was back in The Pitts, she was reminded of the kindness her fellow handmaiden had shown her. Agnes wondered how her ally was coping under Nushka's control.

'I will rescue you, Kayla. You and all the others. Your soul will find its way to the Land of Milk and Honey, I will make sure of it.'

Thorn turned around, offering his hand and embracing her briefly.

"Trust no one except Lilith or me. I don't know how this will unfold, but I will not allow the Gods to take you from me as revenge for my role in this," he whispered so low she could barely make out his words. Agnes nodded into his chest before pulling out of his embrace, staying close.

A shield of fire blazed at the bottom of the staircase behind them, blocking off the entrance to the dungeon and sealing them inside. All around her, the trapped souls and immortals cringed, melting back into the shadows of their cells, many trembling in fright, others begging to be spared.

"Do not fear! We are here to free you," Lilith announced.

Admetos raised his hand before him, fire dancing amongst his fingertips. "It is true. I have been freed and reunited with my power, and they have come to do the same for you."

Footsteps sounded. Only a few at first, then many, as if The Pitts had been alerted to their presence and were now stampeding down the stairs to claim their next victims.

"We don't have time to waste. You each need to take a sip from this," Thorn exclaimed, holding up the vial of tonic, "and we can heal you."

He hurriedly approached the first cell, reaching through the bone cell doors, offering the vial. The powerless God's nostrils flared.

"Orion, you know me, I am here to help," Thorn urged, shaking the vial gently in offering, his arm fully extended through the bone bars now.

"The last time we drank a tonic, it poisoned us and left me like this. I'm lucky to be alive thanks to yours and Lilith's betrayal!" Hunched over, he broke out into a coughing fit.

Admetos moved to Thorn's side. "This will work, brother, blood of my blood. I swear on our father's life. It shall heal you, just as it has healed me. Please," he begged. "Drink it."

"Are you on that traitor's side?!" Orion croaked in disbelief, hobbling on unsteady feet towards the bone bars, but staying just out of reach.

Admetos glared at Thorn. "That wretch can burn in The Pitts for all I care, but what he says is true. The tonic and the witch's spell will heal you," he promised, placing a hand over his heart.

Orion shifted uneasily, the heat of the stone floor Agnes knew all too well likely causing further pain and damage to his already blistered feet.

"And what do you want in return?" he asked suspiciously.

Thorn straightened, his arm remaining outstretched, the tonic still on offer. "I have no right to ask anything of you, but if you choose to, I need everyone's help to defeat Nushka and her army before the universe is beyond saving and all that my father created was for nothing."

The heat of the dungeons caused Agnes's head to whirl, nausea suddenly surging. She took a step forward to Thorn's other side and placed a hand at his back, just as much to steady herself as it was a show of support.

229

Lilith stepped up on her other side, surveying Orion with empathy. "We have wronged you and all the others, and for that we are deeply remorseful. But you and I want the same goal—to make a better world for all mortal and immortal kind. Work with us and together we can create it," she promised, her tone soft and calming.

Orion took the vial from Thorn and sniffed at it incredulously.

"What else do I have to lose that I have not already lost?" he asked, taking a small sip of the vial before coughing and spluttering. Shakily, he handed the vial back to Thorn, glaring at him as he did.

Thorn turned his back on the old God and moved to the next cell. Thankfully, the Goddess in the neighboring cell had seen and witnessed all that had partaken and approached the bone bars on unsteady feet.

"I hope you know what you're doing, Thorn. Nushka will not go down without a fight," she croaked, grasping the vial from him and drawing it to her lips. After a moment of hesitation, she took the smallest of sips, then thrust the vial back into Thorn's hand, a disgusted look upon her face.

Thorn offered his thanks, repeating this process as he progressed down the row of cells, some Deities more reluctant than others to partake of the tonic.

Lilith, standing by Thorn's side once the final God had received their tonic, unraveled the tiny scrap of parchment and together, they began reciting the spell prepared by the High Witch.

"Apokatastíste ti dýnamí sas.

Spáse tis alysídes sou.

Apokatastíste ti dýnamí tous.

Apokatastíste ti dýnamí sas.

Spáse tis alysídes sou.

Apokatastíste ti dýnamí tous."

On and on they chanted as demons and all manner of beasts threw themselves at the fire shield. Admetos sent wave after wave of his power into the protective shield as ghouls and peuchens tried relentlessly to break through. Their roars and screams echoed throughout the dungeon.

Like grains of sand in an hourglass, each chant renewed a fragment of the Gods' power, their auras slowly growing brighter and brighter. Agnes wrung her hands, anxiously flicking her gaze between the fire shield and the God by her side, brow slick with sweat as they droned on and on.

"Thorn, we need to get out of here," Agnes murmured, but the God ignored her, focusing his energy fully on the spell they were casting. Both Thorn and Lilith were visibly paling, and she silently prayed for their renewed strength.

A flash of a shadow followed by a barbed tail whipped through the fire wall, narrowly missing knocking Admetos off his feet. The first being to penetrate the barrier. Admetos groaned as he poured out more of his power, the moans of the beasts behind turning frantic as the temperature in the room became stifling. The world around Agnes began spinning, her vision blurring as she gripped one of the bone bars to maintain her balance. She didn't know how the immortals had survived so long in these wretched conditions. It felt like just yesterday that she had endured being trapped in her corporeal form in one of these very cells, until a small show of kindness had helped draw her from the depths of despair.

The ground shuddered beneath their feet. The roars from the other side of the barrier grew louder as the monsters became more enraged. The moment Admetos's shield waned, they would seize their opportunity and storm the dungeons in search of blood.

"Apokatastíste ti dýnamí sas.

Spáse tis alysídes sou.

Apokatastíste ti dýnamí tous."

Lilith and Thorn's chanting grew louder, the tang of magic filling the air.

"Apokatastíste ti dýnamí sas.

Spáse tis alysídes sou.

Apokatastíste ti dýnamí tous," they continued, throwing everything they had into the spell.

Around them, the magic worked its way through the Deities, the potion and the spell complementing each other, allowing the Gods' strengths and powers to unleash from wherever they had been suppressed or locked deep within. Their panting grew, and some swayed on their feet, as if the restoring of such energy was too much to handle so suddenly. For others, the hope and feeling of change brought gloriously bright grins and set a fire in their gaze. In a wave of bright light, their auras grew like brightly burning stars, illuminating the dimly lit, reprehensible conditions of the dungeons.

One by one, the cell doors were ripped from their hinges as Deity after Deity regained the full strength and might of their powers, claiming their freedom. Shouts of excitement rang out alongside sighs of relief as their wounds began to knit together and color returned to their faces.

"Thank the fucking stars," Thorn panted as he slumped against the side the bone cell where Agnes stood.

On Thorn's other side, Lilith leaned her forehead against one of the bone bars, grasping her hands around two of them to steady herself. Leeched of all color, Agnes was surprised the Goddess was even standing given how drained she had been before they had even entered the dungeon. Agnes wondered what toll this would take on the siblings and how long it would be before both Deities were at their best again. Neither were in any state to walk onto a battlefield.

A scream echoed through the dungeon as Admetos fell to his knees with a crash of metal on stone. Panting and struggling to lift his head, the shield of fire waivered. Agnes shouted in warning, but not soon enough, as a ghoul plunged through a crack in the barrier and leapt upon the God of Fire, driving its blade right through his heart.

Blood pooled on the floor as Admetos's body slumped fully to the ground with a thud, his eyes devoid of light and life.

"No!" a Deity screamed, emerging from her cell, shock and grief etched across her face. She raced to Admetos's side, piercing a shard of her own ice through the ghoul, impaling him against the ground. As the ghoul writhed, trying to free itself, Agnes grasped her hands over her ears to drown out the shrill screeches.

A wave of dark magic whipped over the head of the Goddess leaning over the fallen God's side, flinging the impaled ghoul and those that had emerged from behind the fallen barrier back into the stairwell. A new shield of darkness and wavering wind erected before them. Beside Agnes, Thorn directed one hand towards the barrier, panting, a bead of sweat sliding down the side of his face as he held on for dear life to the bone bar beside her.

"Thorn!" Agnes cried, the world suddenly clearer. "We need to get out of here!"

On Thorn's other side, Lilith wrapped an arm around him to help support him. Biting on her lip, she looked around frantically, for who or what Agnes didn't know.

The Gods rallied around them, and Agnes gnawed on her lip, uncertain if their freedom now spelt her doom.

"Aria," Lilith screamed. "We need to save Aria and destroy Nushka," she cried.

Around her, Gods were already disappearing through portals of their own creations. It felt naive to hope that they had left to aid the cause.

"Lilith," said a God who, even among the immortal Deities, appeared as if he could be one of the ancients. "Where are we needed?" He spoke in an unhurried, even tone, resting a hand upon her slumped shoulder.

Lilith released a sigh of relief, Thorn echoing the sentiment despite his breathless state. Agnes clung to his other side, offering the only comfort she could. Around them, around twenty Gods huddled in beside the ancient immortal, allowing him to take the lead as if he were the authority figure in their Deity hierarchy.

"Phineas," Lilith said a little breathlessly. "Thank you for staying," she cried, silver lining her eyes.

The ancient one softened his gaze. "You came back and you helped us, even when it would have been far easier not to. The debt is paid. All is forgiven," he claimed solemnly.

Lilith's bottom lip quivered. "Thank you."

The remaining Gods and Goddesses around them moved in, offering her small but encouraging nods. Meanwhile, Phineas sent a wave of ancient magic at Thorn's shield, sending a tremor through the dungeon floor. The cracks in Thorn's shield, knitted together with glowing light.

Thorn slumped back against the dungeon bars, losing his hold on the shield as Phineas's renewed strength effortlessly replaced it. Color started flushing his cheeks as he rested. His ability to recover so quickly amazed Agnes to no end.

"Where are we needed most?" Phineas asked Thorn, tilting his head slightly.

"Alearia," Thorn panted. "We have raised an army of souls who march on Alearia as we speak to try and save the last of the living mortals in the Kingdom. From there, we intended to divide and march on the other Kingdoms in the hopes of saving their people from Nushka's dark army as well."

Phineas nodded, weighing the new information. The Gods around whispered their thoughts and concerns amongst themselves.

"And Nushka? Where is she? And Aria?"

"The last I saw of Nushka's power, she was attempting to breach the Afterworld with a portion of her army. She may still be there, but more than likely she has returned to the Land of the Gods upon realizing we had escaped. For all I know, she may be planning to return here to check on her prisoners. It is more than likely word has spread to her by now of intruders in the dungeons," he said, brow furrowed.

"Half of us shall travel home and cut off the army's head where is rests," Phineas said with a wicked grin that was so at odds with his calming persona. "The others shall travel to the mortals' aid."

He spoke for the rest of them, and the other Deities nodded in agreement. Agnes didn't miss the lust for blood shining in many eyes.

Thorn straightened, his breathing more even. Behind them, the woman who had run to Admetos's side held her head low as she rose from the ground, tears streaming silently from her narrowed gaze.

"This is all your fault!" the Goddess screamed, launching herself at Thorn and Lilith, but Phineas caught her by the arm. "Let me go!" Hatred burned in her narrowed eyes as she tried and failed to pull out of his grasp.

"Admetos made his choice, Chiara," Phineas reassured her. "Now we must go. Before we run into any more trouble."

Beside them, two portals opened; one to a land of light guarded by Nushka's finest; the other to a darkened Alearia, where giant oak trees were set alight, snake dragons haunted the skies, and an army of the dead battled chimera and ghouls.

"Thorn, you lead the charge to Alearia. Lilith, you're with us," Phineas commanded, leaving no room for discussion.

Lilith and Thorn met each other's gaze, Lilith's brow slightly furrowed. Agnes straightened as Thorn grasped her hand. Taking a step back, Thorn allowed the ancient one to divide them into groups, the beasts thrashing against the barrier, desperate to sink their teeth and talons into their next victim.

"Chiara is my younger sister, I imagine she has a score to settle with Lilith and I," Thorn whispered in her ear before adding, "Regardless, stay with me, my love."

After wishing Phineas luck as he hurriedly strategized with his group, Chiara, who craved and arguably deserved vengeance more than all the others, was counted amongst their numbers. Thorn turned to embrace Lilith, whispering something indiscernible in her ear before briefly setting eyes upon their small team and crossing his arms in front of his chest.

"We need to work together. We aim for the castle where any remaining mortals will be seeking refuge. The town will be long gone by now," he said, the group of Gods and Goddesses nodding their heads in agreement, Orion amongst them. "Let's go." He gave a curt nod, signaling the end of his short speech and, one by one, their small legion stepped through a portal into a Kingdom that no longer felt like home.

"Welcome to Alearia," Agnes stuttered as her feet set upon sludgy, snow-covered ground.

Anastasia

The dark clouds thundered overhead as the war raged on. Cursing her clunky armor, Anastasia ran through the snow, skirting around towering oak trees and the marching army, headed for the front of their company. In the distance, her comrades in arms were already in the thick of the fighting. Swords clashed against the mighty jaws of the chimera, and the sinister teeth and barbed tails of the snake dragons that had been her undoing in life. Her fists clenched at the sight of them, the memories of her final moments haunting every step as she drew nearer.

After slipping and regaining her footing more times than she could count, she pulled up short, eyes wide as she beheld the unfolding clash of mythical beasts against the army Thorn has raised. The last legionnaires charged into the throng as soon as they hit the battlefield. Up ahead, she caught a glimpse a familiar blonde braid whipping through the air, its bearer facing away from her as they moved to aid a small-statured female who faced off against a chimera, each of its three heads eager to make a meal of them. Anastasia's breathing hitched as her sister disappeared.

Resuming her pace, Anastasia drew her sword and sprinted forwards, sliding beneath a raised peuchen tail, then dodging the slash of a ghoul's clawed fingers. She parried a blow and twisted, slicing the head off her attacker as she sprinted onwards, fearlessly plunging into the familiar dance, her weapons an extension of her arms. All that mattered now was finding her family and her mission.

'What I wouldn't give to be able to shape shift or access my fire wielding gifting again. A dragon that could not die or a gifted army of the dead ... now that would have been an incredible sight. The beasts wouldn't have stood a chance.'

As she dove deeper into the battlefield, weaving between friend and foe, there was no end to the fighting in sight. A dilapidated castle— the place she had called home, now succumbed to an unimaginable war— towered over them from a few thousand feet away; a steep hill of beasts and souls attacking each other without mercy in between. Where the ground leveled out at the base of the castle, the fighting was at its thickest. Peuchen attacked from the skies, beheading one legionnaire after the next, sending them back to the Afterworld. Chimera attacked from the ground, ripping limbs from bodies that fought on despite the pain each soul must have endured.

"Alecia!" Anastasia bellowed, desperate to get her attention as the gap between the two sisters grew. But her calls went unanswered, her words swallowed amongst the screams, roars, and clangs of steel.

A hand from behind clamped upon her shoulder and she ducked down and swiveled, sword singing. Iron met iron as Anastasia's sword met Thorn's a moment later, the rebound shuddering through her arm, causing her to grit her teeth.

"Holy Gods!" Anastasia hissed. "I could have killed you!"

Thorn snorted. "I don't think so, little Queen." His face grew stern as he stepped around her, thrusting his sword into an oncoming assailant taking advantage of her turned back. Anastasia jumped and turned, her sword slicing through the air before cutting off the head of a chimera, the lion sending a spray of blood across her armor. The beast dropped to the ground as Thorn withdrew his sword, the life draining from the eyes of its remaining two heads.

"Thanks for the help," Anastasia yelled across the cacophony of sound.

Thorn nodded. At his back, Agnes severed a peuchen's barbed tail just before it could hit her lover in the back.

Thorn's feral grin reached ear to ear. "That's my girl." He saluted her and Agnes beamed.

"Less talking, more fighting, thank you very much," she yelled, turning to watch their backs.

Around them, ten or so other Gods came to their army's aid, slaying the beasts with such ease they may as well have been crushing ants. They fought mostly with their magic: fire, ice, water, and earth. But some, like Thorn, preferred to use physical weapons, whether to save their strength or embrace bloody vengeance, Anastasia could only guess. Either served their purposes just fine and Anastasia took a moment to thank the universe that they were there and apparently healed of whatever magical disease had plagued them. The chance of making some difference in this war was slightly higher, though she wouldn't have turned down the aid of a hundred more Deities.

242

"We need to get to the castle, that's where any survivors will be seeking refuge," Anastasia called to the God of War. "But first, we need to find Alecia. She's just up ahead." She pointed, her gaze darting everywhere until it settled upon a flash of blond braid that whipped through the air.

"Your wish is my command, *Queenie*," he smirked before grabbing her by the arm and flinging her behind him, sandwiching her between him and her sister. She was momentarily stunned. A wave of darkness erupting from the God of War had her trying to take a step back, but she bumped hard into Agnes. When the air cleared, so was the path to her sister, the peuchen attacking her reduced to cinders.

Anastasia blinked, mouth agape.

Alecia turned, taking in the pile of ash blanketing the ground, her eyebrow quirked as she raised her head to meet Thorn's gaze. The girl who had been fighting beside her flung her head back, embracing the momentary reprieve before throwing herself back into the fray.

"Well, you took your sweet time getting here, God, but I sure as The Pitts am glad to see you here," Alecia grinned.

Thorn scoffed, leading the group to her sister's side, flurries of ash caught in the wind.

"I'm glad to see your sword skills weren't overexaggerated *and* that you haven't given up and returned to the Afterlife already" he rebutted.

Alecia rolled her eyes. Around them, the fighting raged on, though any enemy that drew near found themselves eviscerated by Thorn's power. Anastasia knew the fighting and prayers on this battlefield gave him strength.

She ran to Alecia's side and, just before she could wrap her arms around her, remembered the sword in her hand and drew short. "Whilst I am to see that you are unharmed, we need to get to the castle and find Cimmeris and the children," she pressed. The closer they got to the castle, the sweatier her palms became.

Alecia clasped her free hand to her shoulder. "Tash, you need to prepare yourself. They may not even be here. If they were lucky, they escaped like you wanted them to do," she spoke gently.

Anastasia pulled out of her grasp. "They are here, I can feel it. Either way there are sure to be others that need rescuing."

Alecia's gaze softened, but she nodded. Anastasia turned eagerly to Thorn, "Can you take the lead and clear the path?"

Another God came to Thorn's side, an aura of arrogance about him in the way he puffed his chest and looked down upon her. "Do Gods take orders from souls these days?" he scoffed.

"I meant no offence," she said, straightening her posture. "We need to save my people before it is too late."

Thorn glared at the God. "Shut it, Orion. Go and make yourself useful and lead the other Gods. Clear the field of Nushka's beasts. I don't want to see one peuchen breathing before we leave here."

Orion's eyes narrowed momentarily, but he grinned wildly. Anastasia couldn't get a read on the God's intentions.

"Consider it done," Orion said. "It'll be child's play. When you inevitably need back-up, send one of your souls to find us."

Her blood began to boil at his smirk, but she held her tongue as the God exploded back into the fray, his sword glowing with the brightness of the sun.

Thorn turned to her. "Ignore him. He's been a pain in my side for a millennium and probably will be for a millennium more. Arrogant asshole. Let's go," he said, taking the lead.

Wave after wave of his dark power plowed a path clear to the castle gates, the three sisters hot on his heals, weapons in hand. Wherever Thorn's power landed, only smoke and ash remained, a wake of death and destruction growing with each step closer to the castle that Tash took. Hope and longing grew within her chest.

29

The Goddess of Blood and Bone

Nushka sat upon the remnants of a throne carved from aged oak wood, the flowers and carvings etched into the top half destroyed, likely by one of her beasts when they had first breached the castle walls. A lightning storm and the lit sconces illuminated the unremarkable throne room.

Nearby, Ilbis, her second in command, sat haughtily upon the top step leading to the dais as they waited on the arrival of their *guests*. Their bait awaited them in the catacombs beneath the castle. She sent the Peuchen King to the Land of the Gods as her proxy, for whenever her newly freed prisoners came out of hiding. He would serve as a distraction. At best, he would relieve her of her enemies. At worst, he would delay the reunion of allies. Either way, he would serve his Dark Queen well. If he was to fall, he was a sacrifice Nushka didn't need to think twice about.

"News of Hyacinth's abduction was the first real sign of betrayal," she said to Ilbis, scraping her clawed fingers against the pitiful excuse for a throne. "It was only a matter of time, I suppose. My siblings were never content to live in the shadows." She paused, contemplating for a moment before continuing. "Though, I did not anticipate this turn of events, or else I would have dispatched my siblings long ago when I had the chance. It is sadly not the first time my arrogance has blindsided me."

Iblis stilled, taking in every word, but wisely refraining from comment. To do so would be insolent and Ilbis wasn't stupid.

"Since news of the betrayal reached my ears, we have rallied our allies and expended all our resources into ensuring the destruction of this world. Our time has not been wasted," she carried on, the scraping of her claws etching new lines into the soft wood. "The protective dome that my siblings constructed was more of a challenge to break than anticipated though." She was talking more to herself than Ilbis at this point, processing the last few hours.

"They took advantage of your good will, My Queen," Ilbis sneered, "and for that, we will make them all pay."

Nushka nodded curtly in agreement.

It enraged her to know that she had been a moment too late to prevent the army her siblings had rallied from marching upon the mortal realm. It angered her even more that her beasts in The Pitts allowed her prisoners to escape. News of the Gods breaking free reached her only an hour ago when she had summoned one of the peuchen guards to report on their captivity. After that, a hastily pulled together game of cat and mouse had ensued, and she had made the quick decision to portal to where she was least expected.

It was from Alearia—a Kingdom that had always been her sister's soft-hearted undoing and the homeland of her brother's lover—that she planned to end her fellow Deities for good. It was Thorn, succumbed to the weakness of love, that she anticipated would come to the rescue of his lover's home Kingdom. With the last remaining heirs trapped deep below the castle, one foot still in the land of the living, she knew her brother and her traitor of a former handmaiden would feel compelled to save them.

A sinister smile spread across her lips as she felt a surge of familiar power coming from the battlefields below.

"It appears our guests have arrived," Nushka chimed with delight as a darkness that called to her own was unleashed.

Nushka rose from the throne and descended the stairs, the shadows extending to the hem of her silken ebony gown brushing past Ilbis as she walked.

"Then perhaps we should greet them like the welcoming hosts that we are?" Ilbis jeered, rising to his feet, following the Dark Queen at a respectful distance.

Nushka ignored him as she approached the arched window, offering her a view of the battle raging below, her dark army serving her well. Emerald eyes flared at the sight of the army of the dead working side by side with the very Kin she had entrapped as prisoners in her dungeons. Wave after wave of magic eviscerated her legions. Nushka ground her teeth.

"The arrival of the army of the dead was a clever move on my siblings' part," Nushka reluctantly admitted.

The very sight of the raised army grated on her nerves, but she turned her gaze from the returned Gods to gaze out upon the raised corpses in disgust as she surveyed the carnage below.

"Once their creators have been eliminated, they will cease to be an annoyance," she hissed, her temper rising.

Ilbis crossed his arms, his aura pulsing with power, eager to be unleashed. Nushka had been saving him for last—a power not even her siblings stood a chance against.

"The fact that they still underestimate you, My Queen, astonishes me," he scoffed, looking down his nose at the unfolding scene below. "As if a handful of Deities and a few thousand undead legionaries could take on the might of your dark army."

Nushka turned to him and tilted her head, weighing her next move. "Let us welcome our guests, as you have suggested."

Glee shone through his bright emerald gaze, the mirror of her own. "I couldn't agree more, My Queen." His feral smile sent a delightful chill down her spine that she could not help returning.

Nushka hummed approvingly as she let her eyes flutter closed for a moment, tilting her head back to breathe in the scent of fear radiating from the field below. Her power pulsated, eager to be unleashed. Releasing a tinge of her power, she sent a surge of darkness through the castle, locating her guests. When she opened her eyes, her shadows whispered to her of the goings-on in the realms.

"It appears our acquaintances are headed exactly where we have set our trap," she said to her second, her gaze darkening with glee.

*

The layout of the castle was so simple it was almost absurd to Nushka how easily her shadows had traced her enemy. Power called to power, as it always did. With Ilbis taking the lead, they navigated down the many stone staircases. The lack of light was a familiar comfort, rather than a hinderance after so many years confined to The Pitts. The absence of her allies and near solitude, however, was a new but necessary evil, having spread her forces so thin. Overthrowing the mortal and immortal realms expended far more resources than she had anticipated. Though, even in her wildest dreams, she hadn't anticipated the far-reaching success of her reign of terror. An achievement that had her feeling invincible.

In the neighboring Kingdom of Quillencia, the edimmu clan had taken control of the city, their clan using the capital as their base from which to deploy their army of terrors. The peuchen forces had launched attacks upon Alearia, though their greatest numbers were sent to Shadows Peak. The Kingdom in the far north was hidden within the towering alpine peaks that were blanketed with snow for most of the year, the entire capital residing within the dug-out channels of the jagged mountains. Balconies jutting from the mountainside were the only sign of civilization to the outside world, though the peaks meant that the Kingdom was enshrouded in shadow for most of the day, concealing the community almost entirely from sight. The treacherous terrain meant that invasion was only possible by air—the city balconies the perfect landing platforms for the peuchen. However, the Shadows Peak giant wolves alongside the shadow walkers' numbers were an unstoppable force, and the peuchen had gained little ground thus far in their attempted invasion. Many of the city's residents were hidden away safely for the time being, barricading themselves within the bunkers through tunnels that were too narrow and therefore impassable for the giant snake dragons. Nushka planned to pay the city a visit once the small issue of the other Gods was dealt with.

The chimera packs were divided between Alearia and Stanthorpe where land travel was relatively easy. It had taken the chimera two weeks to secure Stanthorpe's capital, the flat expanses of its plains making invasion almost laughably easy. The Kingdom's legionnaire numbers were so severely depleted after the battle of Alearia that only new troops were left to defend the women and children. The Dark Queen had shown a generous degree of mercy, however, allowing many of the residents to live in exchange for a lifetime of slavery to Nushka's dark army.

Whispering voices pulled Nushka from her musings and she stilled, wishing Ilbis could speak telepathically as the peuchen could. He moved to her side, trying his best to keep his footsteps light, which was near impossible with his imposing presence.

"How would you like to proceed, My Queen?" he asked quietly.

Nushka smiled broadly, revealing jagged teeth as she detected her brother's smokey wood scent.

"I think it is time you showed our guests exactly why you are my second in command," she grinned. Vengeance was so close, she could almost taste it.

"Do you have anything special in mind, My Queen?" Ilbis asked, eyes glimmering with feral delight.

"I think we'll start with the traitress bitch who's sure to be by my darling brother's side. Then we'll move onto Thorn. He needs to learn a valuable lesson about love and loyalty. Perhaps the two can be combined into one pretty package of revenge. What do you think?"

Ilbis chuckled quietly. "I think they are in for a world of hurt. Nothing brings me greater joy than exploiting the weakness that comes from love. That obnoxious prick won't know what hit him."

Nushka breathed deeply, savoring the moment. "Nothing smells quite as good as revenge. By all means, Ilbis, lead the way. We mustn't keep our guests waiting," the Queen said, an arm outstretched towards the dungeons in invitation.

Up ahead, the whispers quietened.

On near-silent feet, Ilbis led Nushka deeper into the heart of the castle. The stone staircase passageway was interrupted by doors with each passing level, with a sconce lit on perhaps every second level they passed *if* they were so fortunate. As they inched closer to the dungeons, her shadows grew increasingly restless at her clawed fingertips. Nushka's hair—a writhing, sentient being—searched for the source of the dark power calling to her own shadows, Nushka's anticipatory delight growing with every step closer to her prey.

The God of War

A trail of bodies had led their small group to the top of the stone staircase. The passageway running through the heart of the castle, leading all the way down to the dungeons and catacombs, sewer streams a level below that. The only way out was through the tainted water, though Thorn highly suspected the barred sewer exit would have been long discovered by their invading enemy and barricaded in, trapping any remaining survivors inside.

The tang of copper clung to the air, the source of it smeared over each of the stairwell's stone steps. Anastasia led the group, eager to find her family... if they remained in the castle at all.

Anastasia arrived at the dungeon door first, the lack of enemy forces during their journey a worrying sign that set the God on edge.

"Come on," Anastasia grunted as she pulled with all her might against the door. It didn't budge. "*Come on,*" she groaned trying again.

Alecia joined her sister and together, they pulled as hard as they could, but the door wouldn't budge. Anastasia began banging furiously on the door, the loud bangs too great of a risk for Thorn's liking. He ran forward and grabbed her arm before she could knock on the door once more.

"Are you crazy?" he whispered furiously. "I know you want to find your family, but we need to be clever about this."

The former Queen glared at him. "They could be in there—it's a good sign that it's locked. Perhaps they're barricaded inside," she cried frantically.

Alecia stepped up to her side and placed a reassuring hand on her shoulder, Agnes stayed back a few paces.

"We'll find them, Tash," Alecia promised her, "but Thorn's right, we need to be smart about this. If we alert the army to our presence, we'll blow our cover and there is no way we'll be able to help anyone then."

Anastasia exhaled deeply, but nodded.

In that moment of quiet, Agnes approached, pressing an ear to door. "Do you hear that?" she asked.

They shouldn't have been able to hear anything through the thick iron door, but Thorn pressed his ear to it all the same. At first he heard nothing and, just when he was about to give up, he heard the faint tapping. Wide-eyed he turned to stare at Agnes.

"You're right. There's something in there."

Anastasia was buzzing on her feet and he moved out of the way so she could try, eager to give her some hope. But only confusion painted her face.

"I can't hear anything," Anastasia said, gnawing on her bottom lip, but keeping her ear against the door hopefully.

"It must be our immortal hearing," Agnes clarified, and Anastasia glared at her.

"Perfect," Alecia interjected as she rolled her eyes. "Another glorious reminder of how everything worked out so well for you."

Agnes's cheeks reddened.

"Perhaps we should focus on the task at hand, rather than making unhelpful comments against the only ones here to help you," Thorn ground out through gritted teeth.

Alecia scoffed, but wisely held her tongue. Thorn cracked his neck, loosening his shoulders. He sent his shadows probing around the door, searching for a weak link, but finding none.

"Get behind me," Thorn commanded. "I'll need to break down the door. Be prepared to fight if the noise alerts anything."

The girls scampered behind him as Thorn rallied his magic. He hoped that whoever was on the other side of that door got the heck out of the way. Drawing upon his wind, he sent a wave of energy slamming into the door. The impact dented the metal, but the door didn't budge. Summoning his shadows to his fingertips, drawing from the well of power deep within, he launched his shadow magic at the door, pouring wave after wave of his energy into the same spot. He grunted from the effort of maintaining the intensity, but after several more moments, the door buckled. Thorn hastily drew his power back within, trying his hardest not to eviscerate whoever awaited on the other side.

The smell hit him long before the dust had settled. Within the cells, the last of a great city remained. Beneath where the fallen door, lay a flattened chimera, each of its three heads lolled lifelessly to the side. Anastasia pushed past him, yelling and screaming as she searched cell after cell for her family.

"Please! Please! Has anyone seen my children?" she screamed, pulling fruitlessly on cell doors.

Agnes moved to stand by his side as Alecia joined the hunt, searching desperately for any trace of their family. The dead were piled at the back of each cell, rats feasting greedily upon their corpses. Many of the living were severely injured with pungent gangrene wounds, their infections likely already spreading into their bloodstreams. The lucky few that were generally well, clung to the bars in disbelief, trauma clouding their eyes.

Agnes stood silently.

"Those poor people," Thorn whispered just loud enough for her to hear.

She nodded solemnly, tears spilling from her eyes, unable to summon the words to convey her feelings.

"Perhaps you should be more worried about yourself, Thorn," a gruff voice came from behind him.

Startled, Thorn whipped around at the sound, unsheathing the sword from his back as he moved.

"Freeze," Ilbis ordered them all as he entered the dungeon, Nushka trailing a step behind, fire burning in her emerald gaze.

Sword held aloft, Thorn's arm stiffened as if frozen to the spot. He pushed against the magic that had taken hold of his mind, but distracted as he was, he had neglected his usual mental shield and Ilbis had firmly cemented his claws within his mind. Beside him, Agnes stood, wide-eyed in shock, unable to move either. Try as he might, he couldn't even talk.

"Well, well, well, I see you received my invitation. How lovely of you to join us," Nushka taunted, her shadows a wild, raging beast at her hands and feet.

Nushka stepped around Ilbis, who smugly looked at Thorn as though he was worse than the scum between his toes.

"My oh my, Thorn, I don't believe I have ever seen you speechless before," Ilbis mocked. "What a pleasant turn of events."

Panic roared within. He scratched and hacked at the claws digging into his mind, preventing him from so much as looking at Nushka or her second the wrong way.

Nushka approached him and caressed his cheek with her sharp claws, drawing blood. "Welcome to Alearia, brother. Though it appears my former pretty little plaything has already provided you with a tour."

'Lilith, where the fuck are you when I need you?'

Nushka licked her lips as she eyed his lover like a delicious meal.

"It has been far too long, Agnes, since you have tended to my every need. I wonder if you warm my brother's bed just as well as you warmed mine?" Nushka said with sickening sweetness, her eyes crazed as she reveled in the moment of having her pray just where she wanted them.

Nushka took a step closer to his lover and ran her tongue along the nape of her neck before pulling back and licking her lips.

"You taste just as good as I remember," she taunted.

His rage grew with each word as he tried and failed not to rise to her pathetic taunts. He had never felt so outmatched and helpless.

"Shall we play a game, My Queen?" Ilbis asked, a sinister grin painted across his face.

Nushka cackled with glee as she clicked her clawed fingers together, her hands steepled in front of her.

"What a wonderful idea."

Her second in command barked a low laugh as he surveyed each of his prey.

"How about a game of 'Ilbis says'?" The second in command setting his predatorial gaze upon Agnes.

"You," he said, pointing. "Ilbis says, drop to your knees."

Panic rose within as his lover did as she was bid, unable to fight Ilbis's order, her knees crunching against the stone floor with only her fighting leathers for protection. The fact that Ilbis could control multiple people at a time was a devastating reflection on the incredible strength of his mind conqueror gifting.

Nushka surveyed his lover with keen awareness. "Very good," she noted approvingly. "Perhaps it is time for Agnes and Thorn to learn a valuable life lesson, wouldn't you say, Ilbis?"

"The one about love always leading to heartache?" he asked gleefully. "Or the lesson about not fucking with the wrong Immortals? That is another one of my personal favorite pearls of wisdom to share."

Behind them, neither the prisoners nor sisters made a sound, as if they were all entrapped beneath Ilbis's mind control. The smell of urine added to the potent mix as someone soiled themselves. The sounds of the raging war filtered down from above, echoing off the stone walls of the stairwell. Thorn prayed that his kin were making good progress and would begin looking for them. They were their only hope of making it out of here alive.

"Shall we wrap those lessons up in one pretty bow?" Nushka said, meeting her second's giddy gaze.

Ilbis stepped close enough to share breath with him. If Thorn had control over his body, he would have seized the opportunity and slayed the beast while he had the chance.

"Thorn. Ilbis says seize your lover by the hair with your right hand and press your dagger to her side with your left, level with her heart."

The world stilled for a moment, a ringing sound echoing through his ears as the order took hold in his mind. Rage echoed through him as he fought with all his might to refuse the order, but his body was no longer his own. He was little more than a puppet. Thorn thrashed his inner shadows against the claws that were entrenched within his mind, trying and failing to regain control.

Thorn dropped his sword, the metal clanging against the stone, his legs moving of their own accord. He took a step to the right until he stood helplessly behind his lover. He grasped Agnes's honey blonde hair with his right hand and thrust her head back so that she looked towards the ceiling. Silver-lined eyes met his own tearful gaze.

Thorn silently begged the stars, the universe, the power within him, to free him from his curse, but nothing happened.

Hair fisted in hand, Thorn's left hand began to twitch and he threw all his mental energy into fighting the order, desperately trying to regain control.

"Press your dagger to her side, level with her heart!" Ilbis repeated, the power zinging through his mind and reinforcing the original order, making it impossible to refuse.

Panic filled Agnes's gaze—the mirror of his own, he imagined. Despite his best efforts, he couldn't refuse the order and, inch by inch, his trembling left hand unsheathed the dagger at his side. Blade in hand, Thorn's hand rose, stopping only when the tip of the dagger pressed into Agnes's side. Just one hard thrust and it would pierce her heart.

Cackling with glee, Nushka delighted in the sight of Agnes at Thorn's mercy.

"Shall I command him to finish the job?" Ilbis enquired.

'No!' Thorn screamed in his mind. The thought of losing the love of his life in such a way was beyond comprehension, even knowing he would see her again in the Afterlife. The future he dreamed for them—the one he had not dared voice—included their future sons and daughters playing in the meadows in the Afterlife, visiting the Land of the Gods on weekends to see their extended kin. But it was all about to be taken away from him and there was nothing he could do.

"Thorn, do you have any last words to say to your beloved before she becomes a permanent resident of the Afterlife?" Nushka asked, a victorious smile on her face.

"Speak," Ilbis commanded of him, loosening the gag order.

Thorn's lips quivered, all the words on the tip of his tongue failing him.

"Make it quick. We will not show you such mercy again," Nushka said, reveling in the pain she caused them both.

Tears spilled freely from Agnes's eyes, shattering his heart into a million pieces.

He wanted to beg Nushka to release them from this torment, but he knew that the gag order would be re-adopted and he would have wasted his chance to speak what was in his heart.

"I will follow you to the ends of the Afterlife and beyond," Thorn whispered huskily, tears trickling down his cheeks, repeating the same words he had pledged to her before. "Where you go, I go. I love you more than all the stars in the sky and I will always find my way back to you."

"I love you," he whispered again.

"End her," Ilbis commanded.

Focusing all his willpower into his arm, he begged the universe to permit him an ounce of self-control. Unable to resist the order any longer, he plunged the dagger straight through his beloved's chest. A piercing scream ripped from his throat as he released her hair at Ilbis's command, the gag order resumed. Time seemed to stand still as Thorn, tears spilling without end, watched the life leave his lover's eyes before she collapsed to the dungeon floor in a growing pool of her own blood, her eyes fluttering closed.

The Goddess of Darkness

Lilith sprinted across the hallway, dodging and leaping over felled peuchen younglings, their giant serpentine spiked tails and unfurled wings filling the hallways wherever their bodies landed. She sent wave after wave of her darkness spearing ahead, leeching the air from their enemies' lungs or shooting shadow magic through their hearts. Phineas, Athena, Adras, and Atlas were close on her heals. Lilith thanked the stars that the younglings were not mature enough to have developed their master's gifts.

Atlas's strength and quick thinking was the only reason they were still alive, having brought down the marble ceiling upon the Peuchen King's head. The weight of the stone had momentarily stunned him, buying them enough time to sprint from the chamber before any more of their kin met the same deadly fate as the others.

Back in the receiving room, Chiara, Adonis, Achilles, Leander, and Rhea had not been so fortunate. Their screams had been snuffed out like candles where they now stood, eternally preserved in stone, having looked into the King's eyes. Despite their chaotic relationship in the past, her sister's passing weighed heavily upon Lilith's shoulders.

Their legion, vastly unprepared for the horror Nushka had left for them as a gift, had walked all too eagerly into one of her traps. The

Peuchen King had been expecting them, and with no sign of the Dark Queen herself, Lilith grew more panicked.

Unnervingly close behind them, the boom of the Peuchen King could be heard as he plowed through walls and corridors that were too small for his giant body to fit. His rage brought down the castle around them, the Gods dodging falling debris and struggling to keep their footing as they sprinted with no real destination in mind. Anywhere away from the terrifying creature with impenetrable scales seemed like a good place to start. The Peuchen King hissed as he followed the trail of bodies Lilith left in her wake.

"Run all you like, Missstresss of Nighttt, buttt I willl catchhh you," he said telepathically.

"Not if I can help it," Lilith muttered breathlessly as she rounded another corner.

The scream of a familiar voice caused Lilith to pause as she risked a glimpse behind her to survey the damage. Adras, pale-faced, was sprawled across the floor, the giant spike of a peuchen tail embedded in his leg. Phineas tried desperately to dislodge it to no avail.

"Run, Phineas, save yourself!" Adras urged.

Athena grabbed the ancient one by the arm and pulled him up. "We need to go," she urged. With a quick plunge of her own dagger through Adras's heart, she freed him of the guilt holding him back as the lady of the hunt blessed the fellow God with the gift of a quick death.

"Run!" she urged again, grabbing Phineas by the arm, Atlas pulling him be the other.

The Gods continued their sprint as the Peuchen King closed the distance. Sensing her wavering strength, Atlas dropped to the back of the company. Unsure of what was happening, Lilith continued her pace, Phineas, and Athena close at her heals. Athena summoned her bow and arrows began flying, piercing through the mouths and eyes of their approaching enemies—the only places their scales failed to protect them. The younglings' muffled final cries were dwarfed by the sound of their falling carcasses.

Behind them, a giant crash sounded and a quick glimpse behind her shoulder revealed that Atlas had brought down the ceiling once more with the hope of buying them more time. Onwards they sprinted, Athena and Lilith firing off arrows and magic, destroying all in their path. If they encountered any mature peuchen, Lilith had no idea what they would do.

Atlas gained ground again behind them. "We need to retreat while we have a moment to summon a portal," he breathlessly advised.

"You're right, we can't go on like this," Phineas replied, panting as he tried to maintain pace with Athena and Lilith. "There will be none of us left to fight another day otherwise."

"Agreed," Athena huffed, taking aim at another peuchen youngling approaching, his tail flicking menacingly.

A quick dive roll allowed Athena to narrowly escape becoming the snake dragon's next victim.

Strength and energy flagging, Lilith tried and failed to summon enough power to open a portal. Chest heaving, she screamed in frustration as her pace began to drop off.

"I can't do it," she cried breathlessly. "I don't have enough strength left to summon a portal."

"Where do we need to go?" Phineas said.

"Alearia," she panted.

As they rounded another corner, five peuchen younglings squeezed into the hallway, directly in their path, forcing the group to pull up short. Athena fired arrow after arrow, but these dragons were smarter than the others, sticking in their pack, reflecting her arrows with their barbed tails.

Lilith retrieved her dagger from where it was strapped to her outer thigh, her gaze flicking between the ancient God and their oncoming attackers. With a mighty crash, the Peuchen King burst through the fallen remains of the corridor behind them.

Panic stricken, Lilith drew upon the final dregs of her power and with one final push, opened a portal to Castle Brandistone. Screaming in pain as she forced her gift beyond its limits, Atlas dove through the portal, followed by Athena and finally Phineas, who grabbed her by the arm just before a peuchen tail could impale either of them. The gateway slammed shut behind them.

*

Pain seared through Lilith's shoulder as she hit the stone floor of the throne room she had visited only once before. Breathlessly, she lay sprawled on the ground, regathering her strength before rising on unsteady legs. She offered a hand to Phineas, whose forehead was bleeding from a nasty gash. He grunted as he took her hand and rose from the ground, his breathing ragged.

Athena crouched low to the ground nearby, her forearms resting on bent knees, the warrior's bow and remaining arrows strapped to her back again. Atlas stood guard at her side, blade in hand as he surveyed their surroundings. Thankfully, the room was otherwise unoccupied.

"What is our next move?" Atlas asked Phineas.

The fact he was looking for leadership elsewhere stung a little. "We need to find Thorn," Lilith interrupted, panic setting in at.

"We need to find the others," Phineas clarified, eyebrow raised.

A flare of familiar magic rippled from within the belly of the castle. *Thorn.*

Lilith's breath caught. "We need to find Thorn. Wherever he is, Nushka is sure to be."

Weak and impatient, Phineas leveled a stare at her. "The fate of all our kin—not just one God—rests on this war. Atlas and Athena will join the others on the battlefield where they are needed most. You and I will go after Thorn."

Atlas and Athena nodded their heads and, a moment later, they were gone.

"Hurry," Lilith urged, grabbing the old God by his arm and wrenching him in the direction Thorn's power led her. A sense of urgency spurred her on, allowing her to draw upon strength she had thought was long spent.

Phineas grunted his disapproval of her manhandling, but followed without complaint. The ancient one was loyal to a fault. Despite all they had done, Phineas would not leave Thorn without support.

Taking the steps two at a time, Lilith raced down the spiral stone stairwell in search of her brother. The pull of his shadows called to her own like a beacon in the night and the dregs of her magic guided her footing. The gap between her and Phineas quickly grew as the elder's reserves began to lag again. The wise part of her gifting told her to ease off her pace—that together they would stand a better chance against whatever was to come. But deep in her heart, she knew time was of the essence. She prayed to the stars she wasn't too late.

32

The God of War

Thorn could see Ilbis's mouth move, hear Nushka prattling her nonsense, but their words lost all meaning. He had lost the love of his life and all hope of creating a family with her. The grief threatened to suffocate him from the inside, his heart fracturing into a million pieces. All that mattered now was that they be reunited.

'I will always find my way to you,' he had promised her.

He prayed desperately to the stars—to anything that would listen—that she found her way back to him. Anastasia and Alecia lifted Agnes's body from the ground, seemingly able to move once more. Perhaps Ilbis ordered their actions, or perhaps they possessed a far greater level of willpower than he.

Thorn wanted to scream at the sisters to stop, to throw himself over Agnes, relentlessly pouring his power into her until her heart had no other choice but to beat again, but he couldn't move. Ilbis's grasp on his mind was far too great and he had no fight left in him to even attempt to break free. He finally understood what it felt like to have loved and lost. The same incomprehensible grief that Anastasia had explained going through was now tearing him apart. As far as he was concerned, the universe could burn. All that mattered was joining his lover in the Afterlife and being soul bonded forevermore.

'Where you go, I go, my love.'

Thorn found himself drawing the second dagger strapped to his belt, his hands moving of their own accord. He felt no fear when the sharp dagger pressed against his throat. He did not fear when his beloved's sisters screamed for him to wake up from his trance. Ilbis silenced their cries as quickly as they escaped, but he couldn't summon the energy to care. His whole body felt numb.

"Give our father my regards," Nushka said in his face.

Thorn met her gaze, her words meaningless to him, his mind already having succumbed to the weight of grief.

Nushka turned to Ilbis, her gaze wild and unrelenting. "Give the order," she commanded.

'The order? What order?' His mind struggled to comprehend what was going on around him. The weight of his arm grew heavy as the blade pressed in ever so slightly against his neck, a trickle of sticky warm liquid dribbling over his hand. The tang of copper wafted up his nose.

*

The Goddess of Darkness

"Give the order," Nushka said coldly, her words echoing up the stairwell. Ilbis's laughter echoed in response.

Raising her mental shields, heart racing, Lilith sprinted down the last few stairs, Phineas trailing a level or so behind, judging from his flagging footsteps. There were few moments in her life that Lilith could recall feeling true terror, but the sight she beheld at the bottom of the stairs made her heart skip a beat.

At the far end of the dungeon, Agnes lay on the floor, all color and life drained from her. Something had gone very, very wrong. Lilith's heart clenched for the pain her brother must be feeling. Alecia and Anastasia silently cried at Agnes's side, their bodies shaking. The stench of the dungeon was unbearable, and flies swarmed the bodies of the deceased. Clinging to the cell bars, frozen at Ilbis's command, stood the Kingdom's last hope of survival.

A foot away from their brother, buzzing with anticipation, Nushka stood mercilessly, ready to take down her sibling. By her side, hands in pockets, Ilbis stood casually. The sight of her brother holding a dagger to his throat was an image that would haunt her all her days.

"Slit your throat," Ilbis commanded.

"No!" She screamed, the raw sound coming from the deepest parts of her heart and soul.

Twin daggers of shadow magic sailed through the air and Nushka turned, failing to raise a shield in time before each dagger found their mark. Piercing screams rang from Ilbis and Nushka as the twin daggers of shadow magic penetrated their hearts with a sharpness and ferocity akin to real iron. The pair dropped to their knees, clinging to their chests.

Lilith stalked toward her prey, retrieving a silver dagger from where it was strapped at her hip and, with a crazed smile upon her face, she slammed the dagger right to the hilt into Ilbis's heart. The hold his mind control spell had on Thorn was severed and her brother's hand dropped to his side.

Thorn stepped forward, anger replacing his grief as he grasped Nushka's writhing hair in one hand and held his dagger to her throat.

"This is for Agnes," he swore, and in one swift moment, he slit her throat. She fell lifelessly to the ground as he released her hair, landing in a pool of blood that was not her own.

Thorn raised his dark gaze to Lilith.

"Nushka does not deserve the luxury of returning to The Pitts!" he spat. "She deserves no mercy."

"Agreed." Lilith stared at him knowingly, a wicked smile spreading across her face as the perfect punishment came to mind.

"An eternity entrapped within her own throne of bone seems a far more fitting end."

Thorn's crazed grin was a thing of nightmares.

The mood quickly changed, the clang of metal on stone sounding as Thorn let go of his dagger. His head dropped as he stared at his blood stained hands. Tears fell freely as he stood frozen, staring at his hands as if under Ilbis's spell. Lilith pulled the dagger from her victim's chest and re-sheathed it at her side, cautiously stepping around her sister's body. She approached her brother and gently took his hands in her own, wiping them clean with a small wave of power.

"I am so very sorry for your loss," she whispered, so quietly that only he could hear.

Thorn's arms dropped heavily to his sides as she released his hands, and The Goddess of Darkness wrapped her arms around him, pulling him into a tight embrace which he did not return. Instead, he rested his head on her shoulder and allowed the well of grief to unspool from within, tears soaking her gown.

"Though your eternity may follow a different path to the one you dreamed of, your journey together is not over. You still have a chance at love and happiness. This is only the beginning of your story. Of that, I am sure."

Epilogue

Agnes

Amongst the rose gardens of a realm that was slowly beginning to feel like home, the inhabitants of the Afterworld gathered. The smell of pine and flowers carried on a gentle afternoon breeze. Beneath the towering sandstone castle, at the front of the crowd, Thorn waited expectantly. Dressed in a perfectly tailored midnight-hued suit and adorned with a modest crown of silver imbued with fragments of departed stars, he was ever the vision of the King of the Afterworld. Beside Thorn, Phineas stood proudly, ready to perform his role as officiant.

After Nushka passed, so too did all her immortal creations—including Hyacinth and the Wendigast witches, much to Lilith's dismay. No longer free to roam the lands of the living, Thorn and Lilith offered her and her kin eternal rest in the Afterworld. After much convincing, Hyacinth had reluctantly accepted their offer and, following her lead, so too did her remaining sisterhood. Even those long since sentenced to The Pitts were granted haven in the Afterworld.

Although it hadn't been the future the sisterhood had dreamed of, the realm created a home for the departed witches. A living treehouse of impressive proportions rose from the belly of a forest in an isolated part of the realm where the Gods hoped the sisterhood could find peace.

The adjustment, according to Thorn, was not going smoothly, though he held on to the hope that time could mend all wounds.

Zeri and the remaining chimera called The Pitts their eternal home, along with Nushka's other creations. Orion—a God that Agnes had little time for—elected himself as King of The Pitts of Moor. As the realm was now free of powerful immortals, none of the remaining Gods objected.

Standing at the end of the candlelit aisle, Agnes gave herself a moment to take it all in as the string quartet began to play, their instruments imbued with the Goddess of Love's magic. The lacy A-line dress and train Agnes wore was created from her mother's memory—a replica of the gown she had worn on her wedding day.

Her mother and siblings had chosen to attend the event, and the heartwarming gesture felt like a step in the right direction as they worked to repair their broken relationships. Anastasia's family were thankfully not by her side, blessedly amongst the living in Alearia. Her sister hoped that they lived long, happy lives, despite how much she missed them. The remaining Gods who had come to their aid during the battle were seated in the front row on the other side of the aisle.

Kayla and Lilith led the procession as her two bridesmaids, dressed in gowns of lilac, though the Goddess of Darkness remained apprehensive over the pastel color choice.

Agnes fidgeted nervously, Amealiana's arm through her own, both in corporeal form.

"It is time, Agnes," her mother said gently.

Agnes offered her a small, nervous smile. "This was not how it was supposed to be."

Amealiana smiled sympathetically. "I am so sorry, Agnes, for the hopes and dreams you have lost. I know how much you and Thorn dreamed of a family and a future together. But the love you have found transcends all others. You will always be soul bonded. Death cannot steal that from you too."

"Thank you," she breathed, her eyes welling with tears.

She threw her arms around her mother, grateful for the chance to do so once again, holding her tightly. Amealiana squeezed her just as tightly in return.

Pulling back, Amealiana smiled softly. "It is time for you to marry the God of your dreams. I am so proud of you, Agnes, Queen of the Afterworld."

Agnes sighed in contentment, taking her mother's arm in her own. With each stride, Agnes grew one step closer to the beginning of her eternal afterlife with the God who'd claimed her heart.

ACKNOWLEDGEMENTS

It takes a team to publish a book and I couldn't be more grateful for the amazing people that support me. Thank you to Chloe Hodge and Aidan Curtis, for turning my stories into art. Thank you especially to Chloe—for your friendship and for helping me to grow as an Author.

Thank you, Bethany Gilbert, for sharing your talent with me and bringing another dream cover to life. I am in awe of your talent and I am so grateful to have you create each of my incredible covers.

Special thanks to Helen Scheuerer for your insightful help with the blurb. I appreciate your friendship and support more than I can ever say.

Thank you, Rebecca Laffar-Smith, for your continuous support and encouragement. Without you this book would not be finished!

Thank you to my husband, for never letting me give up and supporting my dream. Thank you for laughing with me when I say I'm taking a break, knowing that writing is as much a part of me as breathing.

Thank you to my darling daughter Lily. Though you are too young to read this book, I thank you for all the times you gave up your spare time to join mummy at the coffee shop so she could keep writing. Thank you for being such an incredibly supportive, compassionate, caring, young lady. I am so proud of you. I love you more than words can express.

Finally, thank you to my readers, new and old. Without you, I couldn't keep doing the job I love. Thank you for sticking with me with each new book release. Thank you for loving my characters just as much as I do. I hope you all loved following Thorn and Agnes's journey.

Thank you to the reviewers and the social media stars for your support and shout-outs. Without you, my releases would never be as successful. Thank you for all your support!

Lastly, thank you to my family, friends, and fellow authors, who encourage me no matter what. My life is so much fuller for having you all in it.

Thank you everyone,

Nattie x

ABOUT THE AUTHOR

Nattie Kate Mason is an Australian independently published author. Nattie also works as a librarian, sharing her passions for reading and writing. She has travelled around Australia with her little family of three, living in various towns and cities. Life is never dull for Nattie and her unique little family. Nature, life, and reading help to inspire Nattie's creative side. You will often find her outside reading a good book whilst enjoying a cup of tea.

The Gods of War & Darkness concludes the Immortal Deities duology. If you loved the series and want to show Nattie your support, please consider leaving a review on social media, Goodreads and Amazon. Each glowing review helps fantasy lovers like yourself to discover Nattie's books.

Titles by Nattie Kate Mason:

The Crowning, a young adult fantasy series:

The Crowning

A Queen's Fate

Heart of a Crown

The Immortal Deities, new adult/dark fantasy series:

The Goddess of Blood & Bone

The Gods of War & Darkness

Visit nattiekatemason.com to subscribe to her newsletter and stay up to date on her new publications and author events.

Follow Nattie on Instagram, Facebook & TikTok:

@nattie.kate.mason.writer

To read about the fall of the Brandistone dynasty, check out The Crowning series, the prequel to the Immortal Deities duology.

The Crowning series features epic fantasy, royal intrigue, sibling rivalry, magic and a dash of mythology, complimented by a strong mental health awareness message. This trilogy has been referred to as "beautifully written", "captivating," "relatable" and "heart breaking" by readers world-wide.

The Crowning - Book I - synopsis:

An heir to the magically gifted Kingdom of Alearia must be chosen. The shape-shifting Prince Alexander is favoured to claim the title. The fire-wielding sisters, Princess Anastasia, and Princess Alecia feel one of them will take the crown. However, the eldest potential heir, Princess Agnes, has other plans. The current ruler of Alearia, Queen Amealiana, a gifted sage, and seer, has a hidden secret that will change everything. Rivalry, magic, betrayal, healing, death, hope. In the pursuit of power, only one may be crowned Heir.

Praise for The Crowning series:

"If you're a fan of scheming princesses, interesting and varied magic, and a healthy dose of family drama, this book may be for you! I enjoyed how Nattie differentiated the various siblings and their personalities. The villain was particularly sympathetic and I could easily understand how and why she turned to evil. I also enjoyed the final contest between the sisters. These things are usually pretty obvious, but I honestly had no idea who was going to win until right at the end. Kudos to Nattie for keeping the suspense going."

Bonnie Wynne, Bestselling Author

"This book had me hooked from the first page – I loved it! Highly recommended read."

Instagram Reviewer

"Wow! What a wonderful ending to a beautiful trilogy. The world building is great, the characters beautifully developed and the story tugs at your heartstrings at every level. There's passion, anger, vengeance and all out war wrapped in a tale of loyalty, duty, trust and unwavering love. You can't help but be invested in the story and laugh, cry, cheer and pray for everything to turn out all right. Read the whole series.

You will love it, I assure you."

Cassidy Reyne, Author